MW00878766

PRAISE FOR THE L]

"The history learned from 'The Liberty Boys,' for instance, was quite as good as that gotten from school books. Above all, the Revolutionary heroes of the 'nickel novel' had a living quality schoolboys often found wanting in their history books."

—Charles E. Tracewell
"Evening Star," May 29, 1950

[*The writers were*] very fastidious about getting the historical facts correct so that his Liberty Boys went through the American Revolution on historically correct adventures."

—*"Dime Novel Round-Up," May 15, 1957*

All that I am or ever hope to be in the line of diction I owe to 'The Liberty Boys.' Three cheers for Dick Slater, and may his overworked knuckles recover!"

—*"New York Tribune," January 15, 1920*

"What are the young boys reading these days? Are they reading ... 'The Liberty Boys of '76?' Well, what ARE the youngsters of today reading of not these idylls of youth? Will somebody that knows the truth of today tell us?"

—*"Arizona Republican," November 27, 1920*

This 2023 edition is a re-publication of the stories first published in 1901 in *The Liberty Boys of '76* nickel novel serials. It has been lightly edited for contemporary legibility.

ISBN: 978-1-945325-78-6

Published by Ornamental Publishing LLC

HARRY MOORE

PEN NAME OF AUTHORS
STEPHEN ANGUS DOUGLAS COX (1863-1944)
AND
CECIL BURLEIGH (1851-1921)

On January 4, 1901, an explosive new action-adventure book series, *The Liberty Boys of '76,* first hit newsstands. This thrilling series didn't just entertain young readers, it also taught them about real historic events and figures from the American Revolutionary War of 1776.

Penning the series were S. A. D. Cox, a former newspaper editor from Illinois, and Cecil Burleigh, an adventure fiction writer from New York.

In the pages of *The Liberty Boys of '76*, Cox and Burleigh transported kids back in time to witness historic battles, meet legendary patriot heroes like Paul Revere and George Washington, and experience the fight for independence from the British Empire alongside the brave, young Captain Dick Slater.

Ever dedicated to historical accuracy, the authors drew heavily from Benson John Lossing's acclaimed 1851 work, *The Pictorial Field-Book of the Revolution*, to ensure their details were correct. They were also well-known visitors at nearby libraries and bookstores, always researching new historical information.

Stephen Angus Douglas Cox wrote *Liberty Boys* adventures for many years, eventually moving on to Humboldt, Kansas, where he published *The Humboldt Daily Herald* newspaper until his death in 1944.

As for Cecil Burleigh, he authored countless adventure stories in addition to *Liberty Boys* over a very long writing career spanning 35 years. He eventually retired to the quiet life in West Nyack, New York, where he died peacefully in 1921.

With this new edition of Cox and Burleigh's most celebrated adventure series, we hope a new generation of young Americans can learn the importance and cost of freedom, patriotism, and American history, just like their great-grandparents did when they were little.

— The Editors

HISTORICAL NOTE

King George of Great Britain wants to continue ruling the American Colonies, but the American people want freedom to rule themselves. Our story begins on July 4, 1776, a little over a year after the American Revolutionary War began.

Four months earlier —March 17, 1776— George Washington's Continental Army successfully drove the British forces out of their imperial headquarters in Boston, and the Royal Navy fled to Canada to regroup and await reinforcements.

Suspecting that the British would try to establish their next base in New York City, George Washington's Minutemen lost no time in constructing many fortifications around the city to defend against a potential invasion.

On July 2, 1776, the feared day arrived. A British armada of more than 400 ships carrying a force of over 30,000 troops landed and set up camp across the harbor on Staten Island. Admiral Lord Richard Howe and his brother, General Lord William Howe had arrived to attack George Washington's Continental Army and conquer New York City!

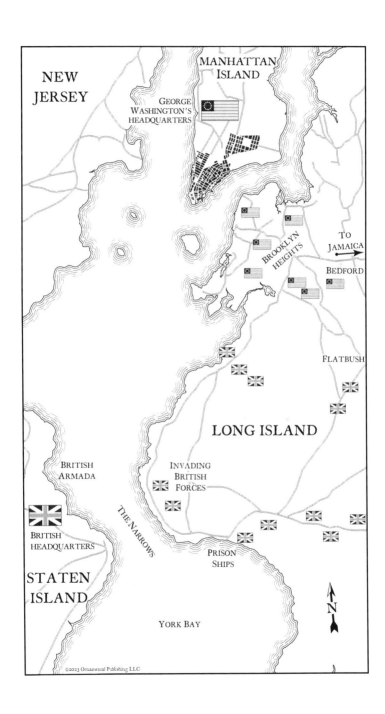

PROCLAIM LIBERTY
THROUGHOUT THE LAND

THE LIBERTY BOYS OF '76

BOOK 1

HARRY O. MOORE

The Liberty Boys of '76

OR

FIGHTING FOR FREEDOM

BY HARRY O. MOORE

CHAPTER I.

A "LIBERTY BOY OF '76."

On the morning of July 6th, 1776, a family of four sat a table in a farmhouse a few miles from Tarrytown, N. Y.

The family consisted of Mr. and Mrs. Slater, their son, a bright-faced, handsome youth of eighteen years, and a daughter, bright and beautiful, aged fifteen. The boy's name was Richard, and the girl's, Edith.

The family was at breakfast, and a pleasant sight the members presented, for they seemed happy and contented.

"What is the latest news of the war, husband?" asked Mrs. Slater, as she poured the coffee.

"Well, the situation remains about the same, wife,"

replied Mr. Slater, who had been to New York the day before, but had been delayed and had not reached home until such a late hour that his wife and children were in bed asleep.

"General Howe has not made any attack on General Washington's army yet, then?" asked Dick, his eyes glowing with the fire of the soldier.

"No; you know it is stated that he has orders to await the coming of his brother, Admiral Howe, who is to try to conciliate the patriots, and get them to lay down their arms and renew allegiance to the king."

"I hope the Admiral won't succeed!" said Dick, his eyes shining.

"And so do I!" declared Edith. "I think we ought to be free!"

"Right, my children," said Mr. Slater. "I stand on exactly the platform adopted by Patrick Henry—'Give me liberty or give me death!' The people of the colonies must be free! They must not go back to the slavery of allegiance to the king!"

Mr. Slater and his two children, as will be seen, were true and earnest patriots. Mrs. Slater was patriotic, also, but she loved her husband, and saw in his attitude great danger to himself, for she was aware that they lived in the midst of a Tory community, the majority of their nearest neighbors being loyal to King George.

They were very bitter toward Mr. Slater, for the reason that he was a very plain, outspoken man, and spoke his sentiments freely, no matter where he was or to whom he might be talking. He was a man utterly fearless, and the threats made against him by his Tory neighbors, which found their way to his ears occasionally, were laughed at. He was not worried a particle, and often when meeting one or more of those same neighbors on the road or elsewhere, he would refer to the matter, tell them he had heard that they had threatened him, and coolly tell them that if they wanted to do anything to him, to do it then and there. His very boldness, however, had saved him, for there was something about him that inspired respect for his prowess. It was not so much what he had done, though he had been a brave soldier of the French and Indian War, as it was fear of what he might do. The majority of his neighbors had seen Hiram Slater when angry, and they knew he was a dangerous man. So, although living in a Tory neighborhood, and being as plain and outspoken as it was possible for one to be, Mr. Slater had so far escaped being harmed.

The bitter hatred which his Tory neighbors felt toward him was to bear fruit soon, however.

"I wish you would be a little more careful what you say to our Tory neighbors, Hiram," said Mrs. Slater. "I am afraid they will do you an injury one of these days. They murder people in these cruel times, and call it some other name."

"Oh, there is no danger, Lizzie," said Mr. Slater. "My neighbors know me too well to do me any hurt. They would get the worst of it."

"But they might not give you any chance to defend yourself, Hiram."

"I don't think there is any danger of anything like that."

"Oh, I don't know about that," said Dick. "There is Hank Scroggs, who is mean enough, I am sure, to do anything. His cowardice is all that holds him back. Then there are Joe Bilkins and Carl Shinker; they are the same kind of men."

"And Samuel Estabrook, Dick?" remarked Edith, demurely.

Dick flushed and looked slightly confused.

"No, Edith," he replied; "Mr. Estabrook is a different sort of man. He is a strong Tory, but I don't think he would do a mean thing, or take advantage of a neighbor because the neighbor differed with him in his views regarding the war."

"Alice is not a Tory," said Edith, with a smiling glance at her brother; "I guess you have converted her, Dick."

Dick flushed, and then laughed.

"That's all right, Sis," he said; "neither is Bob Estabrook a Tory. I wonder if you couldn't explain why? He's been over here considerable, and may have told you his reasons for taking the side of the patriots."

It was Edith's turn to blush now, and Mr. Slater laughed. "That is all right, Edie," he said; "Bob is almost old and big enough to go into the army, and I would rather he would fight, if he fights at all, on the side of Right and

Justice than on the side of a tyrannical king!"

"Bob is a fine boy," said Mrs. Slater.

"Of course Bob's a fine boy," said Dick. "I haven't a friend I think more of than Bob, and I'm sure that if he fought at all, it would be for the cause of freedom, and not to help perpetuate the slavery of the colonists."

"And so would Alice!" smiled Edith.

"Yes; I think she would," agreed Dick, smiling and blushing.

Dick had finished his breakfast by this time, and rising from the table, he walked to the door, which was open, and glanced out.

"Yonder comes a horseman, riding at a gallop, as if in hurry," said Dick. "I am going to hail him. Perhaps he may have heard what was done in Philadelphia the Fourth. I am anxious to know whether Congress declared for liberty."

"That's right; ask him, Dick," replied the youth's father.

Dick hastened out to the road, and called to the man as came up:

"Have you heard what was done at Philadelphia the Fourth, sir?"

The man reined up his horse, and looking at the bright, handsome-faced youth with interest, replied:

"Yes, my boy, I have just come from New York, and they had just received the news there that the Declaration Independence was adopted and signed, and that now it is to be war to the death. The people of the Colonies will free from the yoke of British oppression, or they will die fighting for liberty!"

"Hurrah!" cried Dick, his face shining with delight. "Father! Father!" he called; "the Declaration of Independence has been adopted and signed, and we are free or will soon be free, which amounts to the same thing!"

"Say you so, my son?" cried Hiram Slater, and he came running out to the road to question the stranger.

When the man repeated his statement, Mr. Slater, like Dick, became excited, and cried:

"Thank God for that! I am glad; and I have high hopes, now, of living to see our beautiful country free from the rule of the king!"

At this instant a body of horsemen, consisting of about dozen men, rode up.

They were the Tory neighbors of Mr. Slater, and were armed with muskets and pistols. As they came even with the horsemen, and with Mr. Slater and Dick, they drew and stopping, glared at Mr. Slater threateningly.

"What is all this noise about?" snarled Hank Scroggs who was the leader of the horsemen.

"Why, haven't you heard, Hank?" asked Mr. Slater promptly, and meeting the fierce gaze of the man unflinchingly, even smilingly; "the Declaration of Independence was adopted and signed at Philadelphia the Fourth, and the Colonies are going to be free and independent!"

"You are a cursed traitor, and orter be shot!" snarled

Scroggs.

"And you are a fool for not wanting to be free and independent of King George, who robs us at every opportunity, and—"

"Treason! Treason!" the Tories cried.

"There is no treason about it!" replied Hiram Slater, scornfully; "Congress has adopted and signed the Declaration of Independence, and I am not now a subject of King George, or any other king!"

"It's a lie!" cried Scroggs, fiercely; "you are just as much a subject of the king as you were before, and the doings of your Congress, as you call it, amount to nothing! In three months' time the king's soldiers will have whipped George Washington's army of traitors, and things will be as they were before this rebellion started."

"Never!" cried Mr. Slater. "Never again will King George, or any king, rule over the American Colonies! We will win in this fight just as sure as that sun rises in the east and sets in the west! We will win, and I thank God for it!"

The stranger, who had brought the news of the Declaration of Independence had withdrawn a few yards, and sat on his horse watching the horsemen closely, and the same time flashing an occasional admiring glance upon the bold man who was thus bearding the Tories.

"There is a brave and noble man!" he said to himself; but he is taking his life in his hands, I should say, in talking thus to those men, who look mean enough, and desperate enough, to commit murder."

Mrs. Slater, having come to the door when her husband went out to speak to the horseman, was still standing there when the band of Tories rode up, and her heart sank with a terrible feeling of fear and misgiving.

"They are in a body, and armed," she said to herself; and I fear they have come here to do my husband injury, what shall I do? He will speak up boldly, as he always does, and they may murder him!"

She listened to the conversation which ensued with fear and trembling, and unable to control herself longer, she now called out:

"Hiram! Hiram! please come in! Don't talk to them!"

"That's right; call your old man in, Mrs. Slater!" cried Scroggs, sneeringly; "call him in before we do our duty, and fill his traitorous carcass full of bullets!"

"Shoot, if you dare, Hank Scroggs!" cried Hiram Slater's voice ringing with defiance, his eyes flashing with the scorn he felt for the Tories. "Shoot, if you like, you coward, but little good it will do you if you should kill me, for the people of the colonies will be free in spite of the snakes in the grass, such as you are, who would murder your neighbors to perpetuate your own slavery! You are miserable cowards and curs! and you yourselves know it! Now, shoot, if you dare!" and the bold man folded his arms and gazed unflinchingly into the faces of the Tories.

Mrs. Slater's fears were well founded. These men, who had many a time been forced to listen to the scathing language of the fearless and outspoken patriot, and who had come to hate him as only men possessed of such miserable natures can hate, had got together on this morning, and had come to Mr. Slater's home for the express purpose of killing him. They had already heard of the signing and adoption of the Declaration of Independence, and this had made them very angry, so they had mounted and, as we have seen, appeared before the Slater home just at an opportune (for their purpose) time, inasmuch as Mr. Slater's words gave them an excuse for doing the dastardly deed they contemplated.

"What is that?" almost howled Scroggs, when the brave patriot had spoken; "do you dare call us cowards and curs? By the heavens above us, you shall die for that! You deserve death, anyway, for being a traitor, and you have sealed your doom! Fire, men! Shoot the traitor!" and with the words, Scroggs raised his rifle, and fired point blank at the breast of his neighbor!

"My God! I am shot!" cried the patriot, staggering backward; "wife!—Dick!—Edie!—I am wounded unto death!" and he would have fallen, had not Dick leaped forward and caught his father, and eased him to the ground.

At the same instant three or four more of the Tories fired at the wounded man, another of the bullets striking him, and one or two just missing Dick.

"Lizzie!—Dick!—Edie!— good-by!" gasped the dying man, and then, as his eyes were closing in death, he, by a

superhuman effort, lifted his head, and raising one trembling hand toward heaven, said: "God, I thank thee!—I
die a free man!"

Then his head dropped, a tremulous sigh escaped his
lips, and the dauntless spirit took its flight.

Dick realized the fact in an instant, and with a wild,
incoherent cry, he leaped to his feet and ran to the house,
followed by the jeers of the Tories, who thought he was
running because he feared they might shoot him.

But they were soon to discover their mistake. In the
body of that handsome, eighteen-year-old youth was all
the spirit and indomitable courage of the father, and leaping past his mother, who stood in the doorway paralyzed
with horror at the terrible spectacle she had witnessed,
Dick seized a rifle, which rested on a couple of wooden
forks nailed to the wall, rushed back out of the house to
the road, and before the startled Tories realized what was
happening, the boy raised the rifle, taking quick aim, and
as the sharp ping! of the weapon sounded, Hank Scroggs
threw up his arms, dropped his rifle, and fell forward
upon the neck of his horse, mortally wounded. The horse
became frightened, and bounded away down the road,
and Scroggs, though fatally hurt, managed to hold onto
the animal's mane, and keep from falling off.

Then, with a wild, inarticulate cry of rage and terrible
sorrow combined, Dick clubbed his rifle and attacked
the other Tories, striking swiftly and surely with the
iron-bound butt of the gun. Such was the fierce energy

of the onslaught, so swiftly and bewilderingly did he rain the blows upon the horsemen, that they were rendered unable to fire upon him, and after three of their number had received broken heads, and one or two broken arms, they hastened to spur their frightened horses away from the vicinity, nor did they stop while within sight of the youth.

He had put the entire band of Tories to flight!

But the husband and father was dead! and the grief of the wife, son and daughter was terrible to witness, and the stranger, who had dismounted, and stood uncovered, was very much affected.

Mrs. Slater was seated on the ground, her dead husband's head in her lap, while on one side was Dick, on the other, Edith.

The three wept for several minutes, during which time the man was silent, and then, as the sobs of the sorrowing ones became more subdued, the stranger spoke comforting words to them, and did all he could to lessen their grief.

Presently, Dick, who was kneeling beside his father's form, lifted his tear-stained face toward the sky, and lifting his right hand, said, in a firm, determined voice:

"My father is a martyr to the cause of Liberty, and I, his son, do solemnly swear that I will devote all my energies to the Cause for which my father died, the Cause he loved so well—the Cause of Liberty! I shall become a patriot soldier, and fight for the freedom of our people. I shall devote my whole energies, give up my life, if need be, to the great and glorious Cause! My father would wish it, and I swear to do it, and ask you, mother, and Edie, and this kind gentleman here, to bear me witness in it!"

"Oh, my son! am I to lose you, too!" moaned his mother.

"No; not lose me, mother. I am simply going to do what father would have wished me to do, and when we have whipped the British and Tories and gained our freedom, I will return to you and Edie."

"You are a brave and noble youth!" said the stranger earnestly; "you are a true type of the 'Liberty Boys of '76.'"

CHAPTER II.

AN INTERESTING CHAPTER OF HISTORY.

AND now, kind reader, in order that you may better understand this story—which is to be a story of the War of the Revolution—I am going to interpolate a synopsis of the war to date. While not strictly necessary to the story, it is so thrilling, so full of interest, that it will well repay the reading:

At the time of which we write—July, 1776—a state of war had existed between the American Colonies and Great Britain for a period of a little more than fourteen months, the first battle of the Revolution—the battle of

Lexington—having taken place April 19, 1775.

The British, angered by the resistance of the American Colonies to the attempt to tax them in order to raise the money necessary to pay off the debts incurred in the French and Indian War, had appointed General Gage governor Massachusetts, and he had taken up his quarters in Boston and carried things with a high hand.

The colonists had become greatly worked up over this and on every side could be heard the thrilling words of Patrick Henry: "Give me liberty or give me death!"

Not all the people took this view, however. There were men who were in favor of remaining loyal to King George and these people were called Tories, the people in favor of establishing a Continental Union and pulling entirely away from British rule being called Whigs.

Companies of soldiers from among the Whigs were formed, and these companies of soldiers were called "Minute Men." They made no secret of the fact that they were ready to fight for freedom at any minute, and General Gage became frightened, fortified Boston Neck, and seized powder wherever he could find it, as he reasoned that if the Minute Men could get no powder they could not do much shooting.

General Gage heard that the people were gathering military stores at Concord, and sent out Colonel Smith and Major Pitcairn with eight hundred men to seize and destroy the stores.

The patriots of Boston were not caught napping,

however. They were watching Gage, and knew of his intentions in time. Messengers were sent out to rouse the people. Paul Revere was one of these messengers, and it was then that he made his wonderful ride, made famous by Longfellow.

When the British soldiers reached Lexington they found a company of Minute Men gathered there. Major Pitcairn, who was something of a fire-eater, and hot-headed, rode up to the Minute Men, and cried: "Disperse, you rebels; lay down your arms!"

But the Minute Men did not disperse worth a cent. They stood their ground, like the brave men they were.

Their commander was John Parker, a veteran of the French and Indian War, and when Pitcairn ordered them to disperse, he said to his brave Minute Men: "Stand your ground! Don't fire unless fired upon; but if they mean to have war, let it begin here!"

"Disperse, ye villains!" again roared Pitcairn; "d—n you, why don't you disperse!" and then being angered by their refusal, he roared out the order to his soldiers:

"Fire!"

The soldiers hesitated. They had more sense than their commander, and had no stomach for firing into the ranks of a band of men who were not interfering with them in any way, but Major Pitcairn drew a pistol and fired, repeating his order to fire in a roar like that of a lion, and his soldiers, not daring to disobey a second time, raised their guns to their shoulders and fired a murderous volley, which killed eight of the Minute Men outright, and wounded ten.

The Minute Men at once returned the fire, and for a few minutes a lively scrimmage raged; but Colonel Smith and his company of British soldiers coming in sight at this time made it unwise to keep up the conflict longer at that time, and Parker, the commander of the Minute Men, ordered them to retire, which they did.

The encounter at Lexington had delayed the British, however, and the messengers had had time to reach Concord ahead of them, with the result that when Smith and Pitcairn reached Concord, the patriots had hidden the stores and ammunition, and Minute Men were gathering from all directions.

The British set fire to the court house, chopped down the liberty pole, spiked a few cannon, destroyed a few barrels of flour, and hunted for the ammunition, but failed to find it.

At about this time, the Minute Men, having increased in numbers to more than four hundred, they attacked the British guarding North Bridge, and after receiving and returning their fire, charged across the bridge and put the British, numbering about two hundred, to flight, they retreating into the village. This incident, and the fact that the Minute Men were constantly being augmented by new arrivals from the surrounding villages, alarmed Colonel Smith, and although he had practically accomplished nothing, he ordered a retreat, and the British soldiers started back toward Boston.

And then began a running fight that was particularly galling to the British. The Minute Men followed them, and kept along at the sides, taking refuge behind hills, and in clumps of trees, and they kept up a constant fire upon the fleeing British.

Major Pitcairn, who had fired the first shot of the Revolution, lost his horse, and with it the gold-mounted pistols, from one of which the first shot had been fired, and those pistols may be seen to-day in the town library at Lexington.

The British threw away their muskets, which impeded them in running, and the retreat became a rout. They finally reached Boston, under full run, and were so exhausted they could only fall down and pant and gasp for breath.

The British lost on this day two hundred and seventy-three, while the American loss was ninety-three.

And thus ended the first battle of the revolution. The British had failed to accomplish what they had set out to do, and had been unmercifully whipped in the bargain, and the patriots were jubilant.

Not so with King George and the British, when they heard the news in England, five weeks later. There was general consternation, and they did not know what to think. That their trained regulars, soldiers who had fought in many a battle, should be defeated by a band of "peasants," as the patriots were termed, was past all understanding.

But the effect of the battle was electrical. From all over New England came the companies of Minute Men, gathering near Boston, until very shortly General Gage found himself and his army besieged by an army of "peasants" to the number of sixteen thousand.

The next encounter with the British was when Ethan Allen and Benedict Arnold, with a small company of volunteers, captured Fort Ticonderoga. They secured, here, large stores of cannon and ammunition, which was needed by the troops at Boston. Soon afterward Crown Point was captured.

On June 17 occurred the memorable battle of Bunker Hill. All know the history of this battle. The patriot army had to retreat, after having used up all its ammunition, but although forced to retreat, the effect upon the soldiers and upon the patriots generally was the same as that of a victory. All were greatly encouraged, and the determination to fight for liberty was strengthened and intensified.

Late that summer an expedition was organized to go into Canada. The army was in two divisions, one under General Montgomery going by way of Lake Champlain, and capturing St. Johns and Montreal, and then appearing before Quebec, where it was joined by another small army under Colonel Arnold. They attacked Quebec in a blinding snowstorm, but the attack failed, and although they remained during the winter blockading the city, in the spring they had to retreat and return, the British receiving reinforcements.

On May 10, 1775, the Second Continental Congress met in Philadelphia, and George Washington was appointed Commander-in-Chief of the Continental Army. He proceeded to Boston, and on the third day of July, 1775, took charge of the Army, then numbering fourteen thousand men.

Washington remained there with his army, keeping the British penned up in Boston, and about the middle of March, 1776, he decided to make the British fight or run, and to that end he fortified Dorchester Heights, overlooking Boston, doing the work in a night, and the sight of the cannon frowning down upon them next morning so frightened the British that their commander, General Howe, hurriedly got his army aboard the British fleet, and sailed away to Halifax. A great many Tory families accompanied him.

Next morning Washington entered Boston, and there were great demonstrations of rejoicing. For eleven months the people of Boston had been compelled to have the British soldiers among them, and put up with their insolence and arrogance, as well as submit to having their houses pillaged and stores lifted of their contents, and it was like getting out of jail to be rid of the enemy.

The following little story we find in the history of the revolutionary War, and give it:

"The boys in Boston were wont to amuse themselves in winter by building snow-houses and by skating on a pond in the Common. The soldiers, having disturbed them in sports, complaints were made to the officers, who only ridiculed their petition. At last a number of large boys waited on General Gage. 'What!' said Gage, 'have your fathers sent you here to exhibit the rebellion they have been teaching you?' 'Nobody sent us,' answered the leader, with flashing eyes; 'we have never injured your troops, but they have trampled down our snow-hills and broken the ice on our skating-pond. We complained, and they called us young rebels, and told us to help ourselves, if we could. We told the captain, and he laughed at us. Yesterday our works were destroyed for the third time, and we will bear it no longer.' The British commander could not restrain his admiration. 'The very children,' said he, 'draw in a love of liberty with the air they breathe. Go, my brave boys, and be assured if my troops trouble you again they shall be punished.'"

Such is the story, and we suppose it is true; at any rate, we know the spirit shown by the boys was in them then, and that the boys of this period are possessed of the same spirit.

It shall be my pleasure to, in the story which follows, detail the doings of some such boys as were those who waited upon General Gage—the "Liberty Boys of '76."

General Howe and his army, after evacuating Boston, and going to Halifax, soon afterward sailed to New York, and were joined there by Admiral Howe's fleet, and by General Clinton. General Washington came to New

York with his army, to keep the British from capturing
the city, if he could.

And this was the situation on the Fourth day of July,
1776, when Philadelphia, throbbing with excitement, the
people thronging the streets, awaited the decision of the
Colonial delegations regarding the disposition that was to
be made of the Declaration of Independence, which was
to be presented by the committee appointed to draft it.

With the adoption of this report would come the
severance, at once and forever, from Great Britain—from
allegiance to King George III.

With the adoption of this report would come Freedom, the most blessed boon enjoyed by man. Why, then,
should not the people throng the streets, crowd around
Independence Hall, and wait in impatient eagerness to
learn whether or not the Declaration of Independence
would be adopted and signed?

In the steeple of the old State House was a bell on which,
by a strange and happy coincidence, was the inscription:
"Proclaim liberty throughout all the land unto all the
inhabitants thereof." In the morning, when the delegations assembled, the old bell-ringer had gone to his post,
leaving his boy below to announce to him when the
Declaration was adopted, so that he might ring the bell
and announce the glad fact. The old man waited all day
long, hardly taking time for his dinner, and as the hours
rolled away and the tidings did not come, he shook his
head, and said: "They will never do it! They will never

do it!"

But they did. Along toward evening he heard his boy clap his hands, and then a voice came up to him: "Ring, father, ring!"

The old man seized the iron tongue and swung it to and fro, and thus were the glad tidings promulgated to the waiting thousands on the streets.

The excitement was intense; people acted as though they were crazy. All night long cannon boomed, the people shouted for joy and the illumination from bonfires made the city as light, almost, as day.

And now, reader, after having given you this synopsis of the situation, I will proceed, in chapter three, to detail the wonderful, thrilling adventures during the Revolutionary War—which really dates from this time—of the "Liberty Boys of '76."

CHAPTER III.

DICK AND ALICE.

"AND are you going into the patriot army and fight for freedom, Dick?"

"I am, Alice. My poor father died for the cause he loved so well, and I am going to place my life at the service of Washington, and will fight till we are free, or until I am killed in battle!"

Dick Slater and Alice Estabrook sat on a rustic bench under the shade of an apple tree in the orchard belonging to Alice's father, Samuel Estabrook.

Three days have passed since the terrible morning on which Dick's father was shot down by the Tories, and when Dick had made such a fierce attack on the murderers of his father, and after mortally wounding Hank Scroggs, who had shot Mr. Slater, had put the rest to flight by attacking them with a clubbed rifle.

Scroggs had died the next day from his wound, and that was about all Dick had heard, save that he had been warned by Alice and her brother, Bob, to be on his guard, as it was possible the Tories would try to get revenge on him for the death of Scroggs.

"Let them try it!" Dick had said, his eyes flashing; "several of those fellows fired upon father, after Scroggs had mortally wounded him; I did not see which one fired, as I was assisting father, and my attention was on him, but some of them did it, and if they attack me I will kill a few more of them on suspicion!"

There was a fierceness in Dick's tones that reminded Alice and Bob of Dick's father; but they did not blame him for feeling as he did.

"I wish papa was a patriot!" said Alice, wistfully. "I cannot understand how he can be in favor of remaining a subject of the king."

"I can't understand it, either, Alice; but, of course, he is honest in his views. He thinks it would be best for the people."

"How could it be best, Dick? Just think how glorious it would be to be able to stand erect, throw your head back, and say, 'I am a free man! I am not the subject of a king, but am the equal of any king!'"

"That would be splendid, Alice! And it will be that way, sooner or later, too! This war has but practically begun. The patriots will never give up and become subjects of the king, now that the Declaration of Independence has been adopted and signed. Nothing short of absolute liberty and freedom; nothing short of absolute severance from British rule will satisfy our people now. I am sure of it!"

"I am sure of it, too, Dick, and I am glad! I hope to one day see my father a free man, even against his wishes at the present time."

"He would like it after he had had a taste of it, Alice, I am confident."

"I am sure of it, too, Dick."

"Well, there is one thing about your father, Alice: He is an honest and honorable man, even though he is a Tory. He is not the kind of man to go out and shoot a neighbor because the neighbor differs with him in his views, as is the case with men of the Scroggs, Bilkins, Shinker stripe."

"No, indeed! My father is just the best man in the world, and honestly thinks it would be best for our people to remain loyal to the king. He would not do a mean thing for the world."

"How comes it that you are a little patriot girl, Alice?"

asked Dick, regarding his fair companion with a look of admiring interest.

Well might he look admiringly at Alice Estabrook, if she was as beautiful a sixteen-year-old girl as ever the sun shone on. The luxuriant, wavy hair, the rosy cheeks, dimpled chin, pearly teeth, perfect nose, roguish blue eyes and tempting red lips, all went to make up a picture such as would delight the soul of any man or boy to look upon.

When Dick asked Alice how it happened that she was a patriot, the beautiful girl looked up into his face shyly, and smiling, said:

"You are responsible for that, Dick."

"I?" he exclaimed. There was a pleased tone to his voice.

"Yes; I have heard you talk a great deal, Dick, when you did not know it—last winter at school, for instance, when you had so many arguments with Joe Scroggs and the other Tory boys, and at other times."

"I remember," said Dick; "I did have a good many arguments with the boys last winter at school."

Dick was like his father in the respect that he said openly and frankly just what he thought, on any and all occasions, and under any circumstances. He was absolutely fearless, and this had caused him to have numberless encounters with the Tory boys as school, and elsewhere, but they always got the worst of it, for although only eighteen years old, Dick was a natural athlete, and was very strong and active. These natural physical qualities, together with his indomitable courage and iron will, made him simply unconquerable, and he had, on one occasion the winter before, thrashed four boys who had waylaid him in the woods as he was on his way home from school. They had at first got the better of the combat, owing to force of numbers, but the youth just simply fought on with terrible persistence and fierceness, and his opponents became frightened at last, and the result was that they finally took to their heels and ran, as if for their lives, with Dick in full chase. The spectacle, had anyone seen it, of one boy chasing four must have been ludicrous, to say the least; and each and every one of the four was fully as large and heavy as Dick. One of the four had been Joe Scroggs, the son of the Tory who had shot Mr. Slater, and Joe had cherished a terrible hatred for Dick ever since the time when he and his three cronies were whipped and put to flight in the woods.

"Then I have heard Bob talk a good deal, you know. He was converted by hearing you, and being with you, and he has talked to me a good deal, as he did not dare to talk to papa, and he seemed to want to talk to someone."

"Bob is all right!" said Dick, earnestly.

"Yes; and he thinks that whatever you say is absolutely right, Dick!"

"And how about his sister?" asked Dick, his voice almost trembling, and his handsome eyes shining as they gazed into the roguish blue eyes of his companion.

The girl blushed, looked down in some confusion, and then lifting her eyes to meet his gaze again, said, in a low voice:

"I think about as Bob does, Dick!"

Dick gave a quick glance around, saw no one near, and slipping his arm around the waist of the unresisting girl, he gave her a hug and a kiss.

"Alice," he said, his voice vibrating with feeling, "you are the best, the prettiest, the sweetest little girl in the world, and I am going to go into the patriot army and fight for freedom with a vigor and energy thrice what it would otherwise be, on account of the fact that your sweet face will be ever before me, urging me on!"

"Oh, Dick!" That was all the girl said, but the tone in which she said it was sufficient for Dick, and he kissed the beautiful girl again.

"Here! Here! What is going on here?" cried a voice, and leaping to their feet, the two found themselves confronted by a stern-looking but rather handsome man, of about forty-five years.

"Papa!" exclaimed Alice, her face flushed and confused- looking.

"Mr. Estabrook!" said Dick, his face flushing also, but he met the stern gaze of the man unflinchingly. The youth was a splendid reader of faces, and instinctively he seemed to feel that back in the stern eyes of Alice's father was a faint expression of amusement.

"I repeat, what is going on here?" remarked Mr. Estabrook, for he it was, and he looked from one to the other inquiringly, and with an apparently stern expression of countenance.

"Did you not see what was going on, sir?" asked Dick, boldly.

"I saw you kissing my daughter, young man!" in a stern voice; "and I ask by what right you take such liberties?"

Dick was an impulsive youth, with the feelings of a grown man, and squaring his shoulders, and taking a step nearer Alice, who stood looking at her father half-fearfully, he looked Mr. Estabrook straight in the eyes, and said:

"You ask by what right I kissed your daughter, Mr. Estabrook? Well, I will tell you: By the right which my love for her gives me!"

Alice gave a quick start; she flashed one happy glance into Dick's eyes; her face took on added color, and her breast heaved with emotion.

"What's that, young man! You, a mere youth, talking of love! You do not know the meaning of the word 'love,' nor can she—a sixteen-year-old child."

"I am no child, papa!" said Alice, so promptly that Dick saw something like the ghost of a smile curl the corners of her father's lips.

"I know I am only a youth in years, sir," said Dick, manfully and earnestly; "but I am a man in feelings, and I think I know the meaning of the word 'love.' I know that I love Alice, Mr. Estabrook. I love her dearly, and I am going into the patriot army to fight for freedom and liberty!—and then, if I come forth from the conflict alive, I am going to come to you and ask you to let me have Alice for my wife! I love her dearly, and—she loves me, I think! Do you not, Alice?" and Dick slipped his arm around the girl's waist, and she looked shyly up into his face, and said:

"I do love you, Dick!" A great look of happiness appeared in the youth's eyes, and he drew her closer, and met Mr. Estabrook's stern look unflinchingly and bravely, but without any show of bravado.

"Well, well! of all the impudence!" that gentleman exclaimed. "To talk that way to me, a loyal king's man! To tell me that you are going into the patriot army, and that when you return, after fighting against the king whom I honor, and to whom I am loyal, you are going to ask me to let you have my daughter for a wife! If that isn't the coolest proposition I ever was confronted with, then I don't know what I am talking about!"

"I don't mean to be impudent, sir," said Dick, earnestly; "I am no sneak, to try and hide my views or intentions from the father of the girl I love, and I ask you, would you not rather have me as I am, than to not know where I stand, or what my intentions are?"

"I will admit, Dick," said Mr. Estabrook, in a voice from which much of the sternness was gone, "that I would rather have you as you are than to have you any other way. I have known your parents many years, and I know that two more honest and honorable people never lived. Your father's word was as good as his bond, and he was as truehearted as mortal man could be! He would stand by a friend to the death. I fought by his side in the French and Indian War, and although we differed in our views regarding the present war, we were the best of friends, and no one regrets the manner of his death more than I—you know that, Dick."

"Yes; I know it," Dick nodded.

"And, as I was saying, my boy, I honor you; and feel that my little girl could not have the love of a more worthy young man. I am, as you know, a Tory; but I am honest in my views, and think it would be better to remain loyal to the king. I may be wrong, and I don't quarrel with anyone for being a patriot. Go into the patriot army if you like, Dick—I know that you will make as brave a soldier as ever shouldered a musket—and when the war is over, no matter which side triumphs, if you return alive, and you and Alice still love each other, I shall offer no objections to your becoming man and wife, after you have reached the proper age, of course. You are too young to think of marrying as yet, and if the war should end in a few months, I shall ask that neither of you speak a word to me on the subject until you, Dick, are twenty-one years old."

"That is all right, Mr. Estabrook," said Dick; "we love each other, but we are willing to wait, and something tells me that the war will not end soon—that it will last several years, and if that is the case, I will be needed in the patriot army, to fight for the glorious cause of freedom!"

Alice now gently disengaged herself from Dick's

encircling arm, and stepping forward, she threw her arms about her father's neck.

"Oh, papa! you have made me so happy!" she breathed. "You are the best papa any girl ever had! and I hope you are not angry because I am a patriot. I cannot help feeling that the people should be free, papa! Dick says they ought to be free, and—"

"Dick has converted my little girl, I see!" half-sadly, but with a smile on his face as he stroked his daughter's hair, and then bent down and kissed the red lips. "Well, I don't know that I blame you for thinking as he does."

"I never tried to talk her into thinking as I do, Mr. Estabrook," said Dick; "she just-"

"I got to thinking for myself, papa," said the girl, "and I made up my mind that the people ought to be free!"

"You are your mother's girl, when it comes to that," said Mr. Estabrook. "She leans that way."

"And I wish you did, papa."

The father sighed.

"I really feel that it would be best to remain loyal to the king," he said; "still, I shall not take it to heart, should the people of the American Colonies prove successful, and gain their independence."

"That's the way to look at it, father!" said Bob Estabrook, who had approached unobserved, and who had heard the most of the conversation. "That's the way to look at it! You'll come around all right yet."

Bob was a jolly, lively youth, good-natured, and

thoroughly imbued with the belief that the people ought to be free. He was filled with enthusiasm, and burned with the fire of patriotism.

He took after his mother, who was a patriot, and then he was a great friend of Dick Slater, and had heard that youth talk patriotism so much that he was the strongest kind of a patriot.

"Ah! here is Bob," said Mr. Estabrook, with a smile; "I guess I will have to retire! The enemy has received reinforcements," and giving Bob a shake as he passed him, Mr. Estabrook turned and walked in the direction of the house.

"Oh, ho! what fun!" grinned Bob. "I was watching you two billing and cooing, hugging and kissing, so as to get a line on that kind of business for my own benefit in future, and I saw the governor coming. He caught you at it! He, he, he!"

Dick and Alice blushed, and looked at each other sheepishly, and then laughed.

"Yes, I suppose you wanted to see how it was done, and then go over and teach Edith, you mean, wicked boy!" said Alice.

Whereat Bob flushed up; and then he grinned, good-naturedly.

"I wouldn't mind it, now that you speak of it!" he said, coolly. "It must be pretty good, the way you two seemed to enjoy it!"

"Thrash him, Dick!" said Alice.

"I have a good mind to!" said Dick. "I would, only I know I would have Edith in my wool when she found it out!"

CHAPTER IV.

THE "LIBERTY BOYS OF '76."

"SAY, Dick, are you really going to join the patriot army, and fight for freedom?" asked Bob, eagerly.

"I certainly am, Bob!" was the decided reply.

"I heard you say so a while ago. Well, one thing you can count on, and that is that you are not going without me! If you go, I'm going, and that's all there is about it!"

"But your father will object, Bob."

"No, he won't; and if he does it won't matter. I'll run away and join the army!"

"Would that be right, Bob?" Dick asked, doubtfully.

"Of course it would. All is fair in love or war!" with a significant wink and a grin.

"I don't think papa would object," said Alice. "He knows how mamma feels about the war, and would be willing for Bob to fight on whichever side he wished."

"I'm going if you go, Dick, and that's all there is about it!" the youth declared, and Dick and Alice felt that he meant it.

"I shall be glad to have you along, Bob," said Dick.

"So will Sis be glad to have me go with you, Dick. I see that very plainly. She wants me to take care of and keep you from being too reckless; isn't that right, Sis?"

"Well, you are pretty reckless yourself," she said; "but perhaps both of you would be less reckless if you went to war together."

"We're certainly going to war together!" declared Bob. Then to Dick:

"When are you going?"

"The first of next week."

"Good enough! I'll be ready to start then."

"Are you going so soon as that, Dick?" from Alice.

"Yes; I will have things so arranged that I can leave mother and Edith by that time. You must come over to the house and see them often when we are gone, Alice."

"You may be sure I will, Dick!"

"Are you going to New York to enter the army, Dick?" asked Bob.

"Yes; straight to General Washington!"

"Hurrah!" cried Bob. "Say, I'm tickled to think we are to go into the army and help fight for freedom! I hope we will be able to do good work for the glorious cause of liberty, Dick!"

"And so do I, Bob."

The three talked for some time, and then, bidding the two good-by, Dick parted from them and made his way back to his own home, which was about a quarter of a mile distant.

The youth's face saddened as he entered the yard and approached the house, the sight of which brought back memories of what had happened there a few days before.

"Poor father!" Dick said to himself; "he died a martyr to his patriotism. Well, I will enter the patriot army and try to do credit to him, and help make the great cause which he loved so well successful!"

Dick's mother and sister were seated in the front room of the house. They were sad-faced, for they had loved the husband and father devotedly; but their faces brightened as Dick entered.

"Where have you been, Dick?" asked Edith.

"Over to Mr. Estabrook's, Edith."

"Did you see Bob?" eagerly.

"Yes, Sis. He is going to go to war with me."

"What! Bob is going to go with you?"

"Yes."

"Going to join the patriot army, and fight against the king!"

"Yes, Edith."

"And his father a king's man! I should not think Mr. Estabrook would let him do so." This from Mrs. Slater.

"But his mother is a patriot, mother," said Edith; "and Mr. Estabrook is not the man to try to force Bob to do anything against his wishes. Bob will be left to do as he likes in this matter, I am confident."

"I think you are right about that, Edie," said Dick. "Mr. Estabrook is a sensible man, and will not try to turn Bob from his purpose, I am confident."

The three conversed together for some time, and then Dick left the mother and sister, and went to his room. He was busy all the rest of the day, getting ready to go to New York the first of the week to join the patriot army.

That evening, at about nine o'clock, as they were seated in the-sitting room talking, there came the sound of hurried footsteps outside, and then the door opened, and Bob Estabrook entered.

"Excuse me for entering so unceremoniously" he said, bowing to Mrs. Slater, and smiling at Edith; "but I have important news for Dick, and did not want to waste any time in stopping to knock."

"That is all right, Bob; sit down," said Dick. "What is the news you speak of?"

"I'll tell you: The Tories, under the leadership of Joe Bilkins and Carl Shinker, are going to attack you, here in the house, to-night, Dick!"

An exclamation of terror escaped Mrs. Slater.

"Oh, what shall we do!" she cried; "they will murder Dick, as they did my poor husband!"

"No, they won't, mother!" said Dick, his eyes flashing; "forewarned is forearmed, you know, and they will get the worst of it, if they try it on! But how do you know they are going to do this, Bob?"

"You will never tell, I know," said Bob; "so I don't mind telling you that father told me. The neighbors know that he is loyal to the king, and one of them let the cat out of the bag to him. Of course, he is your friend, and he told me, so that I could come to warn Dick."

"I am much obliged to you and your father, Bob; but do you suppose they will really dare to try to do anything?"

"Of course they will! They want revenge on you for shooting Scroggs, and they will be expecting to take you by surprise, you know."

"Well, they'll miss it there."

"You must not remain here to-night, my son!" cried Mrs. Slater. "You must leave, and at once."

"What, leave home? Run away from a gang of cowards such as are those fellows? Never! Mother, I will stay here and fight them to the death! I have father's rifle and pistols, and plenty of ammunition, and I shall stay and fight them!"

"Good for you!" cried Bob, admiringly; "and, Dick, got a surprise for you!"

"A surprise for me?"

"Yes."

"What is it?"

"I'll show you—see here," and going to the door, he gave a shrill whistle, and a few moments later a dozen youths of about Dick's and Bob's age filed into the house and bowed to Mrs. Slater and Edith.

Dick recognized the boys at once. They were the sons of the patriot neighbors, and were all schoolmates of himself and Bob.

"Well, well! this is a surprise, sure enough!" he

exclaimed, and then he shook hands with the boys.

Each of the newcomers carried a rifle, and in a belt at their waists were pistols, while hanging at their sides were the powder-horns and bullet-pouches.

"You boys look as if you were going to war!" said Dick, when the greetings were over. "What means this warlike demonstration?"

"We have come to help you fight the Tories to-night, Dick!" said Bob.

"I suspected as much!" said Dick.

"We will make them wish they had stayed away and attended to their own business," said Bob.

"That's right," said Mark Morrison, a handsome youth of eighteen years.

"We will give them a lesson that they won't forget soon!" from another of the boys.

Dick's face glowed with pleasure.

"You are friends worth having," he said. "I am glad you have come; and now, when those cowardly Tories come here to-night, thinking to surprise me, they will themselves be surprised!"

"So they will!" grinned Bob.

"What time will they be here, do you think, Bob?"

"About midnight, I think was what the Tory said that told father about it."

"Very well; we-will be ready for them!"

The boys talked the matter over, and arranged their plans. The house was a story-and-a-half structure, and

Dick told his mother and sister to go to bed at the usual hour in one of the upstairs rooms, while he and his companions would remain downstairs in readiness to greet the Tories when they put in an appearance.

This was done, and the boys extinguished the candle and sat in the darkness, talking in whispers. They did not know but the Tories might come earlier than was expected and did not wish to betray their presence in the house. The door was bolted, so that they could not be taken by surprise.

It was about half-past eleven when the boys heard the sound of footsteps outside.

"They are coming!" whispered Dick.

The boys grasped their rifles with nervous energy, and listened intently.

The footsteps approached the house, and it was easy to know from the sound that there were a number of men outside.

The footsteps ceased presently, and the boys heard a fumbling noise at the door.

"Who is there?" called out Dick, in a stern voice.

There was no reply, but utter silence for a few moments, and then Dick called out once more:

"Who is there?"

"A friend; open the door," was the reply, in what was evidently a disguised voice.

"You are a liar, you Tory scoundrel!" cried Dick, defiantly; "go away, now, at once, if you know when you are well off!"

An exclamation, sounding like a curse, was heard, and then a gruff voice called out:

"Open the door, Dick Slater, or we will smash it in!"

"If you smash that door, you will sign your own death warrant!" retorted Dick. "There are a number of us in here, and we are armed. Go about your business, and thank your lucky stars that we were willing to let you escape!"

"Bah! you can't frighten us away with such words, Dick Slater!" came back the reply. "We are going to drag you out of the house and hang you to one of the trees in your own door yard! That is the way we intend serving all traitors!"

"Go ahead and do it, then, if you think you can!" replied Dick, defiantly.

"That's just what we will do!"

There was the sound of shuffling feet outside, and Dick took advantage of the opportunity, and told his companions to be ready to fire at the word.

"They will batter the door down," he said; "and as soon as the door gives way, I will give the order, and we will fire a volley into the midst of the scoundrels! If a second volley is necessary, draw your pistols and fire."

A few moments later the sound of rushing footsteps was heard, and crash! something heavy came against the door, which shook and creaked under the impact.

"They have found a heavy sill, or something of the kind,

are using it for a battering-ram," said Dick. "The door will go down next time; and be ready to fire if it does!"

The boys replied in low tones that they would be ready, and then, crash! came the battering-ram against the door a second time—this time with success, for the door burst from its hinges, and fell inward to the floor.

A wild yell of triumph escaped the lips of the Tories and they started to leap through the open doorway into the house. At this instant, however, the word "Fire!" in a clear, ringing voice was heard, and the crash of a dozen or more rifles as they were discharged almost raised the roof!

Immediately following the volley from the rifles, came a chorus of yells of pain, rage and astonishment, and these were followed by groans and curses.

Dick had all the qualities of a good general. He seemed to realize, intuitively, that it would be an easy matter to put the enemy to complete rout by charging out upon them, and he gave the order to do this.

He leaped through the open doorway the first one, and after him came the other boys, pell mell, anxious, now that their blood was up, to get at the enemy. In a moment they were upon the astonished Tories, who, although numbering fifteen at least, immediately took to their heels and ran for their lives. The shock of the volley from the rifles had shattered their nerves, and the fierce charge of the youths had been too much for them; they could not stand their ground. Doubtless they thought they were being attacked by a regiment of soldiers.

"Go it, you cowards and murderers!" cried Dick, scornfully; "run, like the cowards that you are—and if you know when you are well off, you will stay away from here in the future!"

The boys were jubilant over their quick and decisive victory. They had put the Tories to flight much quicker than they had anticipated being able to do.

Dick stationed a couple of the youths for guard duty, while he and the others went to work to mend the broken door.

Mrs. Slater and Edith were delighted when they learned that not one of the boys had been injured in the least, and they were glad when Dick told them that he did not know whether or not they had killed any of the Tories.

"They deserved killing, whether we killed any of them or not!" said Bob. "They would have hung Dick, had they got hold of him."

"True," acknowledged Mrs. Slater; "but it is a terrible thing to have to shed human blood in this manner!"

"All is fair and right in war times, mother," said Dick.

"We are fighting for our rights, for liberty, and I do not think it is wrong to shoot our enemies. If we hadn't shot them, they would have shot us."

After the door had been repaired, Mrs. Slater and Edith returned to bed, and the boys sat up the rest of the night, talking of the war.

And there in the house that night, the boys, after due consideration and discussion of the subject, decided to get up a company from among the boys and young men of the neighborhood, elect Dick captain, and go down to New York and offer their services to General Washington.

This would take a couple of weeks, as they would have to hunt around a good deal to find a sufficient number to make out the company, but it was decided to do it.

"And what will we call ourselves, when we have organized our company?" asked Bob. "We must have a name."

"We will call ourselves the 'Liberty Boys of '76!'" said Dick.

CHAPTER V.

DICK AND THE COMMANDER-IN-CHIEF.

THE great General George Washington sat in a room at his headquarters in the city of New York.

He was in a deep study.

The British were threatening to attack the American Army on Brooklyn Heights, and as General Howe had fully twenty-five thousand troops, while Washington had only eighteen thousand, the problem of how to hold the Heights was a serious one.

And hold it he must to retain control of New York, for Brooklyn Heights commanded New York, the same as Bunker Hill commanded Boston.

While the General sat buried in thought an orderly

entered, and bowing, said:

"A young gentleman to see your excellency."

"Ah!" abstractedly; "who is the young gentleman, orderly?"

"I don't know, sir. He did not give his name, but said, 'Please tell General Washington that a Liberty Boy of '76 wants to see him.'"

'A Liberty Boy of '76,' eh? A good title!—yes, a very good title, indeed! Show him in, orderly."

The orderly retired, but returned soon, and ushered a handsome youth of about eighteen years into the room. "How do you do, young man?" remarked General Washington, pleasantly. "To whom am I indebted for this call?"

"My name is Dick Slater, your excellency. I am a patriot, and the son of a patriot who was killed a short time since by Tories. I wish to offer my services, and I have out here a company of youths like myself, all of whom wish to join your army and help fight for liberty. We call ourselves the 'Liberty Boys of '76.'"

The eyes of the commander-in-chief shone with pleasure.

He stepped forward and extended his hand.

"Master Slater—Dick," he said, feelingly, "I accept the offer of yourself and company of Liberty Boys with pleasure; and I will say, while I am on the subject, that the Cause of Liberty cannot fail when such brave boys as yourself will get up companies and come and offer yourselves to be used for the purpose of fighting for freedom!

We cannot lose; we must not lose; we will not lose!"

There was a determined ring to the voice of the great man, and Dick felt that he stood in the presence of a wonderful man, a genius for generalship such as the world has never seen—and probably never will see—excelled.

"Will your excellency review my company of Liberty Boys?" asked Dick. "They would like to see you and have you see them."

"Yes, indeed, Dick," was the prompt reply, for, like the majority of great men, he was courteous and kindly; "march them past and I will review them."

"Very well, your excellency; and thank you, sir."

Dick saluted, and started to withdraw, but Washington said, "Wait a moment," and Dick paused.

The commander-in-chief looked at Dick long and searchingly. He seemed to be sizing the youth up, and undoubtedly the verdict as a result of the scrutiny was satisfactory, for he said:

"After I have reviewed the company of Liberty Boys, and they have returned to their quarters, you will please report to me as soon as possible, Dick."

"Here, sir?" asked Dick.

"Here."

"Very well; I will lose no time in reporting to your excellency," and with a bow, Dick left the room and the house.

"A likely-looking youth!" murmured Washington, when Dick was gone; "I believe he might succeed where men have failed. I will give him the opportunity, at any rate."

"I wonder what the general wants to see me about?" thought Dick. "Well, it doesn't matter; whatever he says for me to do, that will I do, or die trying!"

Dick returned to the company of Liberty Boys, his face glowing.

"The commander-in-chief will review our company, boys!" he cried; "get ready at once. And we must do our best and make as good a showing as possible!"

The boys were eager and excited, but fifteen minutes later they were ready, and leaving their quarters they marched up the street past the commander-in-chief's headquarters. General Washington was out on the stoop, and as Dick and his company of "Liberty Boys of '76" marched past, the great man waved his hand in a graceful salute and smiled. Dick returned the salute, and then the Liberty Boys returned to their quarters, and Dick hastened to return to the commander-in-chief's headquarters.

He was shown into Washington's presence as soon as he gave his name, the orderly having been instructed to admit him at once.

Washington nodded and smiled.

"You have a splendid company, my boy!" he said. "It is my prophecy that your 'Liberty Boys of '76' will make a name for themselves before this war ends. If I had ten thousand such troops, I could bid defiance to Generals Howe and Clinton."

"I am glad you liked their looks," said Dick, simply;

"they are each and every one ready to lay down their lives for the great cause of freedom."

"I believe you," the general said; and then he looked searchingly at Dick, and asked:

"If I were to say to you, Dick, that I would like to have you enter upon a dangerous undertaking, an undertaking in which your life would be threatened at every turn, would be in danger every minute, what would be your reply?"

"That you have only to command, your excellency," was the prompt response. "I am here at your service, and if I go where my life pays the forfeit, it will be lost in a noble cause. I am ready to go anywhere, undertake anything, risk everything. You have only to tell me what it is that you wish me to do."

"Nobly spoken!" exclaimed Washington, in admiration. "Dick, you are a true Liberty Boy, and I am going to honor you by sending you upon a difficult and dangerous, nay, desperate undertaking. If you should succeed in doing what I wish done, you will have rendered me an inestimable service, and perhaps saved the lives of thousands of patriot soldiers."

"I will do my best to succeed, sir," said Dick, his handsome face lighting up with enthusiasm.

"I know you will, my boy; and I hope and trust you will succeed."

Then the commander-in-chief looked down at the floor for a few moments, as if in deep study.

"Dick," he said, slowly and deliberately, "just outside the Narrows lies the British fleet, under Admiral Howe, and on the southwest shore of Long Island, just off which lie the ships, is General Howe's army. The British outnumber us considerably—just how much I do not know, but wish to—and I wish you to go over to Long Island, and make your way, if possible, into the enemy's lines, and find out not only how many troops they have, but what their intentions are. I fear an attack on Brooklyn Heights, and I would give much to find out when the attack is to be made. Do you think you could do this for me?"

"I am willing to try, your excellency!" said Dick, promptly.

"You are a brave and noble youth," said Washington; "and I dislike to send one so young on such a perilous undertaking. I have already sent two of the best spies in the Continental Army, and they have not returned. They were captured, undoubtedly, and were likely shot or hanged. And such would be your fate, my boy, if you were captured and thought to be a spy."

"I am ready to go, sir," said Dick, firmly; "I am willing to risk my life for the good of the great Cause; am willing to, if need be, lose it. I think, though, your excellency, that a boy like myself would be less liable to be suspected of being a spy than a man, and I have hopes that I may be able to penetrate into the enemy's lines and escape death as a spy."

"I had thought of that, my boy; in fact, that was the

reason I decided to send you. Two of my best spies, both men grown, have failed, and I thought that a boy might be able to do what those men have failed to accomplish Then you are willing to undertake this dangerous work?"

"Not only willing but eager to undertake it, your excellency! I wish to do something that will be of moment, something that will be of value to the patriots' cause."

"Good! and thank you, my boy. I shall let you go upon this dangerous errand, but it would be well to wait till evening. Come to me at four o'clock, and I will give you a letter of introduction to General Putnam, who has charge of the forces on Brooklyn Heights. He will give you further aid and instructions."

"Very well, your excellency; I will return at four." Then Dick took his leave, and returned to his company of Liberty Boys, and told them of his good fortune—as he considered it—in being chosen by the commander-in-chief to go over onto Long Island to act as a spy among the British.

They were excited, and each and every one thought exactly as Dick did regarding the matter. They were proud that their captain should be chosen by the commander-in-chief to go on such a dangerous and important errand.

"The general couldn't have done better than to pick on you, Dick," said Bob, earnestly; "you will succeed, and find out all about the British, if anybody can do so!"

Bob thought there was nobody quite the equal of Dick Slater.

"I hope to be successful," said Dick, modestly.

"You will be; I am sure of it!" said Bob. "How I wish I could go with you," he added, wistfully.

"Do you think you would like to be a spy, Bob?" asked Dick.

"I know I should like it!"

"Well, if I am successful the commander-in-chief will probably keep me at the same kind of work, and he would no doubt then be willing to give you work in the same line, Bob."

"I hope you will be successful, then."

At a quarter to four that afternoon, Dick bade good-by to his Liberty Boy friends, and went to General Washington's headquarters. The general gave him the letter to General Putnam, with instructions regarding the best route to take to reach Brooklyn Heights, and then Dick took his departure, the cheery words of encouragement from the commander-in-chief ringing in his ears for a long time.

It was almost dark when Dick finally reached the headquarters of General Putnam, and when "Old Put," as he was familiarly called, read the letter, he looked at the youth before him in astonishment.

"And you, a mere boy, are going to try to penetrate the British lines and spy on them!" he exclaimed. "My boy, you are going on a dangerous errand."

"I know that, sir," was the quiet reply.

"And yet you are not afraid?"

"I go where duty calls me, sir. If I were very, very much afraid, I would go just the same. I have but one life, but I am willing to risk, and if need be lose, it in fighting for the great Cause of Liberty."

"Bravely and nobly spoken!" said Putnam, admiringly, and he gazed into the frank, bright face of the youth with interest. "I will give you all the aid in my power—which this instance is confined to directions as to the best course for you to take in trying to reach the British Army, down on the south shore."

"Give me such information as you can," said Dick, simply, "and I will start at once."

"But you must have something to eat and drink first. You can eat while I give you your instructions."

"A piece of bread and a cup of water is all I care for, sir."

Food was brought, and Dick ate heartily, for he was a boy, and a healthy one with a good appetite, and by the time he had finished he knew all that General Putnam knew regarding the location of the British Army, and regarding the best way in which to go in order to reach the army.

It was now quite dark, and he left Putnam's headquarters, and with a good-by to the orderly who had accompanied him through the American lines, he plunged into the darkness and set out afoot in the direction in which he knew was the British Army.

"Let's see; General Putnam said it was about five miles, as near as he could judge, to the British lines. Well, I ought to reach there in a couple of hours, anyway."

Thus thought Dick, as he made his way along. He was headed for Flatbush, and thought that he might learn something there regarding the British.

Dick reached Flatbush, but decided not to tarry there long, as he saw a couple of companies of redcoats walking about. He was questioned by the captain of one company, who asked him where he lived, and Dick said, "Out in the country."

"Well, it is time you were getting home," said the officer "you are liable to be gobbled up by the rebels."

"I am not afraid," said Dick, quietly; and then he drew back the skirts of his coat, and said:

"See; I have my father's pistols, and if the rebels try to catch me, I will shoot them!"

The officer gave a start, and looked at Dick suspiciously.

"See here, my young friend, you are pretty young to be sporting pistols!" he exclaimed; "that savors more of the style of the sons of the cursed rebels than of the son of a king's man. Who are you, and where are you going?"

The British soldiers now came crowding around, and they all regarded the youth suspiciously.

"He's a young rebel spy and you may be sure of it, captain!" said one. "He looks it; see what a wicked eye he has!"

"It isn't any more wicked than yours!" retorted Dick, who was a youth not to be awed.

"Better take him prisoner, captain!" advised another,

"He is too saucy, altogether!"

"I am going to do so," said the officer; "disarm him, men!"

But Dick was not disposed to submit to capture thus early in his career as a spy. Simulating a fear which, strange to say, he did not feel, although surrounded by British soldiers, Dick drew his pistols from his belt, and said:

"Here are my pistols; take—their contents!" and as he spoke thus he quickly fired the weapons point blank in the faces of the officer and his men; then striking right and left with the weapons, the bold youth broke from among the soldiers, who were surprised and thrown into disorder by being fired upon by the boy, and before they realized it, he was clear of them, and running down the street like the wind.

"Don't let him escape!" howled the officer, who had been wounded in the cheek by one of the bullets, and was in a rage as a result; "don't let the cursed rebel spy escape! Shoot him dead!—fire, men, fire!"

The soldiers had recovered from their amazement and disorder, now, and raising their muskets, they fired a volley. At the same instant the fleeing youth fell forward upon his face, and a wild shout of joy went up from the British soldiers.

They thought they had killed the youth, but they were mistaken. By a fortunate accident, Dick stumbled and fell just as the British were pulling the triggers, and the result was that he went down just in time to escape the hail of leaden pellets, they going above him. Then he leaped to his feet, with a shout of defiance, and springing around the corner of a house, disappeared from the sight of the amazed and discomfited British.

CHAPTER VI.

WITHIN THE BRITISH PINES.

"THAT was a close call," said Dick to himself, as he ran rapidly out of the village and into the country and darkness; "it was a close call, but a miss is as good as a mile. I rather think I astonished those fellows a bit, anyhow!" and the youth smiled grimly.

"Gracious, though," he murmured; "the British are crowding up close to the American positions! I hope I will be able to discover something of importance, and get back to General Washington with the news."

The youth struck into the country road which ran almost due south, and followed it for about a mile, when hearing the sound of horses' feet behind him, he stepped aside and took refuge in the edge of a field.

"I'll reload my pistols while waiting for those people to pass by," Dick thought, and he proceeded to do so.

As the horsemen drew near, Dick listened intently, and soon decided that it was a company of British soldiers.

"They are not the fellows I had my encounter with back

at Flatbush, however," he decided; "they are laughing and joking at a great rate, while the fellows I met would be talking in a different strain.

"They have been on a foraging expedition," he said to himself, as he heard their remarks; "and are on their way back to the main army."

A bright idea struck Dick.

"I'll follow them," he decided; "and in that manner I will be led direct to the British Army."

The horsemen were riding at a leisurely gait, so it was not a difficult matter to keep up with them, and Dick was glad they had come along.

A mile further, and the horsemen reached the main encampment of the British, and Dick had been forced to stop a quarter of a mile back, as he was aware of the fact that he could not enter the lines by way of the road without being challenged, as there would be pickets out.

"I'll take a circuit out and around, and see if I can slip in unobserved," thought Dick, and he proceeded to put this move into practice.

"I am in a dangerous neighborhood," he said to himself; "but no matter; I will find out how many men the British have, and what they intend doing, or die trying!"

The youth made his way through the underbrush, which was quite thick here, and by listening intently at intervals he was enabled to locate the sentinel, and by the exercise of considerable woodcraft he succeeded in slipping through between two of the pickets, although they were within a few yards of each other—were so close that they were talking to each other, in fact.

The youth had just managed to get across the line, and was congratulating himself, when he stepped on a dry twig, and it broke with a loud snap, sounding trebly sharp in the stillness.

"Halt! Who comes there?" cried both sentinels.

Dick paused, but made no reply.

"Who comes there?—quick! or we fire!" cried the sentinels, and knowing they would keep their word, Dick leapt away through the underbrush as rapidly as he could go in the darkness. He made considerable noise, and the sentinels, locating him as well as they could by this, fired, the reports of the weapons arousing the encampment almost an instant.

The bullets came so close to Dick that he heard their whir, but he did not care for that. They had not found lodgment in his body, and he was satisfied.

He was confronted with a difficult problem now, however: He was within the British lines, and the entire encampment was in an uproar. It would be a difficult matter to escape detection and capture; in fact, it would be almost an impossibility, and the youth thinking quickly and to the point, decided upon a bold stroke:

He would walk boldly into camp, and pretend that he wished to join the British Army!

"I don't know whether I can make it win or not," the youth murmured; "but I'll try it. A bold game is often successful where any other kind would fail."

Then he advanced rapidly and walked right up to the main body of the British.

"Hello! who are you?" exclaimed an officer, staring at Dick.

"I'm a boy," replied Dick, coolly.

"So I perceive; but who are you and where did you come from?"

"Me? Oh, my name is Sam Sly, and I live up the other side of Bedford."

"Ah, you do? Well, how in blazes did you get through our lines?"

The British soldiers had gathered around, and were listening to the youth, and watching him with interest, the camp fires throwing out sufficient light so that it was possible to see very well.

"Why, I walked through."

"Ah, you did? Didn't you see any sentinels?"

"No; but I heard some!" and Dick grinned.

"Was it you who caused the disturbance out there just now?"

"I guess it was, sir. At any rate, a couple of your sentinels fired at me, and I heard the sing of the bullets as they went past."

"You did? Were you not scared?"

"No."

"You weren't?"

"No; there was no use to get scared after the sentinels

had fired and missed."

The officer gave Dick a shrewd look.

"Well, you are right about that," he said; "but it is seldom that such a philosophical head is found on such young shoulders. What did you want here, anyway, that you should be slipping into our lines in this manner?"

Dick saw that the officer's suspicions were aroused, and he made up his mind that he would have to be very circumspect if he succeeded in disarming suspicion.

"I wasn't slipping into your lines," the youth said, quietly.

"You were not?"

"No."

"What were you doing, then?"

"I was walking into your camp, with no attempt at secrecy, when the sentinels heard me and fired upon me."

"Indeed? What were you coming into camp for?"

"I wanted to offer my services as a soldier in your army."

The officer studied the face of the youth closely.

"You did, eh?" he remarked.

"Yes, sir."

"You are loyal to the king, then?"

"Oh, yes, sir!"

Dick's nature was so open and frank; he had such a native dislike for falsehood that even though he felt that he was justified in telling an untruth to deceive the British, yet the falsehood came so stumblingly from his lips that the keen-minded officer became suspicious.

"You are sure of that?" he asked.

"Yes, I am sure of it," the youth declared. Then, feeling that some decided statements were needed, he added:

"Just give me a chance to prove it, is all I ask! If I don't do as good fighting as any of your men, then you can shoot me!"

"You look to me somewhat like a rebel!" the officer remarked, coldly, and Dick began to see that he was in for trouble. This was made more of a certainty a few moments later, when the company of soldiers with whom Dick had had his encounter at Flatbush an hour or so before, rode into camp.

The captain had his face tied up in a silk handkerchief, and the instant his eyes fell on Dick, he pointed at him, and cried:

"Tie that young scoundrel up! He is a rebel, and, I am confident, a spy! He shot me back at Flatbush an hour ago, and wounded one of my men so badly we had to leave him behind! Tie the young scoundrel up!"

The officer who had been questioning Dick looked at him and smiled coldly.

"What have you to say to that, my loyal young friend?" He accented the "loyal."

"What have I to say to that?" coolly.

"Yes."

"Simply that the gentleman lies!"

Dick spoke so calmly, and in such a matter-of-fact way, that the British officer gave a gasp of astonishment.

"Do you mean to say you did not shoot the captain,

back at Flatbush, as he says?" he asked.

"Oh, no; I don't mean to say that. I mean that he lies when he says I am a rebel."

"Oh; you still claim to be loyal to the king?"

"Yes; and wish to join the army, and fight for him."

The captain had dismounted by this time, and now advanced and confronted the youth threateningly.

"Have the young traitor tied up at once. Captain Park," he said; "he is a rebel spy, and I am sure of it! Put him in the prison-pen along with the other two spies who were recently captured, and see how he will like that!"

Dick almost gave a start. He remembered that General Washington had said he had sent two men to spy on the British, and they had not returned. The words of the wounded captain would indicate that the two men in question were held prisoners, and the youth's heart leaped when he thought that perhaps he might succeed in rescuing them, and aiding them to escape and return to New York.

"They will have some valuable information, and if I can free them, and we can get away, I think I will have done more than the commander-in-chief expected I would be able to do."

"The captain is mistaken," he said aloud; "I am not a spy, but a loyal subject of the king. However, I suppose you will do as you like with me. I cannot prevent you."

"Why did you shoot me, then?" asked the wounded captain.

"Because I thought you were going to hang me for a spy at once, without giving me a chance to prove my loyalty, and I decided to escape if I could, and join the army."

"I believe it will be best to give him a chance to prove his loyalty to the king," said the other captain.

The fact of the matter was that there was bad blood between these two officers on account of a love affair with one of the pretty, buxom Dutch girls of the vicinity, and Captain Park was secretly glad Dick had shot the captain in the cheek, and he hoped the wound would spoil the gallant captain's beauty.

"Oh, all right; do as you like!" half-snarled Captain Frink. "I hope he will turn out to be the rankest kind of a rebel, and shoot you full of holes!"

With this amiable remark, Captain Frink stalked away, followed by an amused laugh from Captain Park.

"I am going to give you a chance to prove your loyalty, young man!" he said.

"That is what I want," replied Dick.

CHAPTER VII.
GATHERING INFORMATION.

Dick was allowed his freedom, and he wandered about, seemingly merely interested by the novelty of the sight of so many soldiers, but the shrewd boy spy was listening to the conversation about him, and treasuring up every word.

The soldiers of the king were not believers in the "early to bed, early to rise" philosophy, evidently, for they did not turn in until after eleven—that is, the majority of them did not.

This gave Dick some little time in which to circulate around and hear what was being said.

"When are we to move on the rebels?" he heard one soldier ask another.

"I don't know," was the reply; "before very long, though, I think."

"We'll eat them up, when we do go after them!"

"Yes; I understand that General Howe says the capture of the Heights now occupied by the rebels will practically end the war, as it will win New York for us at once, and force Washington to retreat out of the city."

"That's right; I wish we could capture Washington himself; that would put an end to the whole business."

"So it would; I wish it, too, as I am anxious to get back home. I don't like this business of being over here and having to fight these bushwhacking rebels."

"Neither do I; but I think that the capture of the Heights of Brooklyn will end the matter, practically."

"You will find that you are mistaken about that!" thought Dick, and then as the two began conversing about home affairs in England, he moved on.

"Who in blazes are you, and what are you wandering

around here for, like a restless spirit?" asked a sergeant of
Dick, a few minutes later.

"I'm just looking at the soldiers," replied Dick, quietly.
"No harm in that, is there?"

"That depends. Who and what are you?"

"My name is Sam Sly."

"Sam Sly, eh?"

"Yes."

"Well Sam Sly, how sly are you?"

The officer chuckled; he thought he was saying something smart.

"Slyer than you think, perhaps!" thought Dick; but
aloud he said:

"I am not very sly. I am a country boy from up Bedford
way, and I have come down here to join the army, and
fight for the king."

"You are loyal to the king, then, are you?"

"Oh, yes, sir."

"Well, that's the way to be. And you want to fight for
him, eh?"

"Yes."

"Jove! I wish you could take my place and fight, and
let me go back to England!" with a dry laugh. "After you
have been in one battle, you won't be so eager to fight for
the king, or anyone else!"

"Maybe not," simply. "I want to try it, anyway, and see."

"Bah! you couldn't fight anything!" sneered a soldier,
who had been drinking a bit more than was good for

him, and who had listened to the talk of the youth with a scornful expression of countenance. "You would run at the first fire."

"Judging me by yourself, I suppose?" remarked Dick, coolly.

A number of the soldiers who sat near and heard the remark laughed loudly at this, and began chaffing the soldier.

"Ha-ha! he was too much for you, Moggsley!"

"The kid is lively with his tongue!"

"He's all right!"

"You had better keep still, Moggsley!"

But the British soldier was of a mean, quarrelsome disposition, especially when he was in his cups, and he became very angry.

"Why, you cursed little whelp!" he cried, leaping to his feet and glaring at Dick in a manner intended to frighten him half to death, but which failed of doing so, as the youth met the look unflinchingly; "I have half a mind to wring your neck! You are altogether too free with that tongue of yours, and for two shillings I would cut it off!"

"Would you?" remarked Dick, coldly; "I don't think you would!"

"Oh, you don't, eh?"

"I do not!"

"The boy is spunky!" exclaimed a soldier, admiringly. "He is gritty!"

"He has enough spirit for a rebel!"

The angry soldier advanced threateningly, and drawing a knife from his pocket, and opening the blade, which converted the knife into a dirk with a blade six inches long, he held it up and smiled in a fiendish manner.

"D'ye see that knife?" he asked.

"I see it!"

Dick was perfectly cool. He felt that he was more than a match, physically, for any king's soldier, on account of the fact that he was a trained athlete, and he did not exhibit the least nervousness.

"Well," said the soldier, fiercely, "I am going to use that knife on you!"

"I'd advise you not to attempt it!" said Dick, promptly.

"What?"

The soldier was astonished at the youth's coolness, as were the onlookers also.

"You heard what I said."

Dick was as calm as ever.

"You say you'd advise me not to attempt it, eh?"

"Yes."

"Why, what would the young high-cock-a-lorum do?"

"He would knock you down!" was the prompt reply.

The soldier laughed hoarsely.

He considered it a rare, good joke that a boy should talk of knocking him down.

"Why, ye little whelp!" he said, scornfully; "ye couldn't knock me down in a week!"

"You try using that knife on me, and see!" said Dick,

quietly.

"Well, that's just what I am going to do! I said I thought of cutting your tongue off, but that would be too bad, I guess; so I will content myself with cutting a piece off the top of each of your ears! That is the private mark which Hank Moggsley puts on people he doesn't like!"

"Have you ever put the mark on anybody?"

"Yes, sirree; on lots of people."

"Defenseless old men, and boys ten or twelve years old, I suppose!"

Dick's tone was scathing, and the laughter which greeted this remark of Dick's made the soldier very angry.

"You insolent young hound!" he hissed; "you do not know what you are doing! Anger me too much, and I will kill you!"

"Try it, you coward, and see what you will get!" said Dick, who had made up his mind to give this arrogant, boastful fellow a lesson.

"Jove! but the boy is gritty!"

"He is a good one!"

"That's right!"

The remarks of the soldiers made the fellow more angry than ever, and when he found his speech—Dick's last remark had almost paralyzed him—he hissed:

"So! you will have it, eh? Well, your blood be on your own head, then! You should have kept a civil tongue, and not been so saucy!"

Then he crouched for a spring at the daring youth.

The soldiers sitting around cried to Dick in warning, but it was not necessary. The youth was watching the angry man, and was ready for him.

As the soldier leaped forward, knife in hand, with a snarling cry of rage and menace, Dick's right arm shot out, and the king's soldier was knocked down with a neatness and despatch that was remarkable, and the force with which he struck the ground caused him to give utterance to a grunt.

And now the soldiers who were witnesses to the remarkable affair were astonished as they had never been before.

Exclamations of wonderment escaped them.

Moggsley was a bad man, and was feared and disliked by his comrades on account of the fact that he was of such a vicious nature. He would as lieve kill a man as not, and had done so on several occasions. It was war time, however, and he had been let go. After the war was over, he would probably be hanged.

Moggsley lay there on the ground, blinking up at the sky, for nearly half a minute.

Then Dick stepped forward and gave him a poke with the toe of his boot.

"Get up, you coward!" he said, sharply! "Get up, and finish killing me, if you are going to do so; I am in a hurry to have the affair over with."

This aroused the fallen man, and caused murmurs of astonishment at the youth's temerity from the spectators.

"You'd better run, young fellow, instead of staying and

making him madder than ever."

"He'll kill you!"

"That's right; you'd better get out while you have a chance."

"What! run from a coward such as he is?" exclaimed Dick, with scorn; "not much! I am not through with him yet! He shall not escape me so easy as all that! The scoundrel has, I have no doubt, murdered defenseless people, and I am going to give him such a thorough thrashing that he will be in no condition to do any more such work for a long time to come!"

The soldier had now scrambled to his feet, and he stood and stared about him for a few moments, as if still somewhat dazed. Then he caught sight of Dick, and it all came back to him.

He gave vent to a snarl of rage.

It sounded like the snarl of a wounded panther.

He leaped toward Dick, knife in hand, his face convulsed with rage and the light of murder.

He would have no mercy on the youth, if he could once get him in his power.

But Dick was not disposed to let this happen.

He disliked all king's soldiers.

He disliked this one more than anyone he had yet seen.

To his mind, Moggsley was worse than a ravening wolf.

So he made up his mind to treat the scoundrel roughly.

As the man leaped forward, Dick jumped to one side. The stroke of the knife, which the fellow made as he came forward, missed Dick by a foot at least.

Then, crack! the youth's wonderful fist took Moggsley on the jaw, and down he went again, with a thud.

A long drawn out "Ah-h-h-h!" escaped the spectators. They were never so surprised in their lives.

That a youth such as was this should floor a grown man like Moggsley was almost unbelievable.

But the evidence was before their eyes.

Moggsley lay there on the ground, looking up at the stars in a dazed way, helpless for the time being.

Doubtless he saw a great many stars not down on an astronomer's chart.

Dick stood there, his arms folded, looking down at his fallen foe.

"Come, come!" he said, sarcastically; "you will never finish me if you don't do better than you have been doing! Get up and try it again!"

"Young fellow, you are a good one!"

"Yes; but Moggsley'll kill you yet! You'd better get away while there is yet time."

"That's what he will do; and it would be a pity, too, to see such a brave fellow die! Get out, and stay away from Moggsley in future."

"I'm not through with Moggsley yet!" said Dick, in the grim, determined tone which was his birthright. "I am not going to let him escape so easily."

"Listen to that!"

"You are a bold one!"

"He has made his words good, though, so far!" Moggsley was stirring now, and the attention of all was turned to him.

He raised himself to a sitting posture and looked around him in a bewildered manner.

"What has happened?" he asked; and then he felt of his jaw, and made a grimace.

"My jaw hurts," he said; "what is the matter with it?"

"That is where I hit you just now," said Dick, calmly. "Get up, quick, and I will give you another in the same place!"

This brought the soldier back to a realization of all, and he scrambled to his feet.

He had dropped the knife when he went down the last time.

He made no effort to regain it.

Doubtless the two attempts he had made to reach the youth, failing each time, had taught him the uselessness of trying to prosecute the attack further at short range.

At any rate, he decided on another course of procedure.

He reached his hand to his belt, quickly, and drew his pistol.

He leveled it at the youth.

There was a fiendish look, a look of fierce joy and triumph, on his face.

"I am going to shoot you down like a dog! you cursed young whelp!" he cried; "die!"

But the wonderful quickness of the youth foiled him

gain.

Dick leaped aside with the quickness of thought, and as he swayed his body downward, and to one side, he struck upward with his arm, striking the pistol arm of the soldier, and knocking the arm upward, so that when the pistol was discharged, the bullet went whistling up in the air.

Then, crack! the youth's terrible fist took the would-be murderer on the jaw, and down he went for the third time.

The spectators stared in open-mouthed amazement.

They had expected nothing else than that the youth would be shot down, but again he had outgeneraled his opponent.

The noise of the pistol-shot alarmed the camp, and officers of the guard came running up to see what was the trouble.

When they learned what it was, they turned on Dick.

"What do you mean by coming into the camp and raising such a disturbance?" an officer asked.

"I didn't raise any disturbance, sir."

Dick was cool and composed.

"You did not?"

"No, sir; that fellow started it himself."

"I don't believe it!"

The officers feared the fellow, as he was an inveterate gambler, and it happened that they owed him considerable in the way of gambling debts, and they did not wish to have to say anything to Moggsley.

"It is the truth, just the same," said Dick; "and I can

prove it by the soldiers who saw the affair from the start."

"Who are you?" abruptly.

"Sam Sly."

"What are you doing here?"

"I am a king's man, and I came here to join the army, and fight for King George."

"Oh, that's it. Well, you have made a very poor start, you have been fighting against the king's soldiers, from the looks of things."

"No; only against one, and he is not a soldier, but a scoundrel!"

"That will do! Go to the supply tent and get you a blanket, and turn in for the night. You have done enough deviltry for the once."

"I don't want to go till I have given this coward the lesson he needs."

"He will be in no condition to fight you; see, he is dazed."

This was really the case, and feeling that he had punished the fellow pretty thoroughly, Dick walked away without another word.

He made a few inquiries, here and there, and presently found the supply tent, and securing a blanket, he lay down, and wrapping himself in the blanket, was soon fast asleep.

CHAPTER VIII.

THE PRISON-PEN.

ONE would have thought that the young patriot spy would not have slept much.

There are not many who, placed in his position, would have done so.

The majority in his situation—a patriot spy in the midst of the British Army—would have been so nervous and frightened that they would not have been able to close their eyes in sleep at all.

But not so Dick.

He was a peculiar youth.

He had nerves of steel, had perfect control of himself, and no feeling of uneasiness came to disturb his mind and keep him from sleeping.

He went to sleep and slept as soundly as he would have slept had he been at home in bed.

Imagination he had none.

No fear of what might happen ever bothered Dick Slater's mind.

He was intensely practical.

It was his way to wait till danger actually threatened, and then meet it as best he might be able at the time.

These peculiar qualifications would make him a splendid spy.

Dick awoke much refreshed next morning, and after

having eaten a good solid breakfast, he felt that he would be in good condition to prosecute his investigations during the day.

Captain Park ran across him at an early hour, and after questioning him further, found him a place in a company of his regiment.

The soldiers did pretty much as they liked, excepting during drill hours.

They wandered here and there, and squads were constantly going and coming from the beach, where they bathed.

Dick went along with one of those squads.

When they came to the beach, Dick noticed several old hulks lying near the shore in a little cove, sheltered from the rougher waters of York Bay, where the British fleet lay at anchor.

"What are those old hulks there for?" he asked of a fellow with whom he had struck up a sort of friendship.

"Those are intended for the reception of such prisoners as we capture when we storm Brooklyn Heights," was the reply.

"Ah! I see; prison-pens, eh?"

"Yes."

"They have no occupants as yet, have they?"

"A dozen or two. You see, we pick up a few stragglers occasionally, and there are a couple of spies in there, too."

"A couple of spies, you say?"

"Yes. They are to be shot in a few days."

"And serve them right!" declared Dick, with assumed fierceness. "The idea of their turning traitor, and working against the king! They ought to be hung!"

"You're right about that!"

"Are they all in the same hulk?" asked Dick, looking at the prison-pens with disguised interest.

"Yes; they're in this one, nearest the shore."

Dick had learned what he wished to know, so said no more just at that time.

When they came in sight of the British fleet in York Bay, Dick asked how dangerous the vessels were.

"Are they all in good fighting trim, and well-manned?" he asked.

"Oh, yes; the ships are all right, and there are plenty of men aboard them," was the reply.

"That is good; there is no danger that Washington and his army of traitors will come down and capture them, then."

The soldier laughed.

"Well, I guess not!" he said.

"There must be an awful lot of soldiers here!" said Dick, presently. "I never saw so many men together before in all my life."

"There are at least twenty-five thousand men in the army that has been landed since the ships reached here from Halifax and England."

"Phew!" whistled Dick; "why don't they attack the American Army at once, and wipe it out of existence?"

"We are going to do so in a few days, now—so I heard the captain say yesterday."

"What day, do you know?" asked Dick, so eagerly his companion looked at him somewhat suspiciously.

"What makes you seem so excited?" he asked, suspiciously.

"Why, I want to be in the fight!" the youth cried. "I wish we were going to attack them to-day!"

"You're all right, I guess!" with a smile. "Well, I know the exact day we will move on Brooklyn Heights, it will be within four days, at any rate."

Four days!

Dick made a mental note of this.

This was important news, indeed!

It was something that General Washington ought to know at once.

Dick made up his mind that the commander-in-chief of the Continental Army should know it very soon.

The youth was determined not to leave, however, after he had at least made a desperate effort to set the spies and other patriot prisoners free, and aid them to escape.

He was not the kind of a youth to go off and leave poor men to their fate.

That fate would be death by hanging, or by bullet, and as he had four days in which to return to the commander-in-chief with the information which he had gained, he determined to take the prisoners with him when he went

Dick went in bathing with the others, and spent a

couple of hours there. He was careful to count the British war-ships and take particular note of them.

He saw that carpenters were at work on three or four and he jumped to the conclusion that the vessels were not seaworthy as they might be—at least some of them were not.

"I wish I could sink the whole fleet!" he thought, and he got to pondering, in the hope that he might think up some scheme whereby this might be accomplished.

It was a difficult problem, however, and he dismissed it finally, as impracticable.

Dick spent the day much after the same fashion as the rest of the soldiers. He saw the soldier Moggsley once during the day, but the fellow for some reason pretended not to see the youth.

The fact was, he was afraid of Dick, and although burning with hatred for the youth, he did not dare show it, but hid it, and awaited an opportunity to strike Dick when he was not looking.

Dick read the fellow correctly, however, and smiled to himself.

"He would murder me if he got the chance," he thought; "well, I won't give him the chance."

"When evening came, and it grew dark, Dick began to grow restless.

He could not content himself to sit by the camp fire and listen to stories.

He was anxious to be away to the old prison-pens made

on the hulks of dismantled vessels.

He was eager to rescue the spies and the other patriots imprisoned there.

Dick got up and sauntered slowly away, looking here and there in the most natural and careless manner imaginable. No one to have seen him would have thought that he was burning with the desire to leap away at a run, and race down toward the water-front to where the old hulks lay. The youth had splendid control of himself.

This was what was going to make him such a wonderful success as a spy.

"Where are you going, Sly?" asked Captain Parks, as he passed where that officer sat engaged in gazing up at the stars in meditation.

"I feel restless, captain," replied Dick; "I will take a little walk before turning in for the night."

"Very well; but don't go far."

"I will be back in a few minutes."

Dick passed on, and as he left the light thrown out by the dozens of camp fires, and as he entered the darkness, a dark form went stealing along in his wake.

He was followed; and the man following him was bent on murdering the youth.

Moggsley had been sitting near the camp fire reading, when he happened to look up and saw Dick leaving camp, and he at once leaped up, and assuming a carelessness he was far from feeling, he followed the youth.

Dick kept on down the road toward the beach, walking

quite rapidly now, for he was where he would be unobserved, was sure, and he wished to get to the old hulk
which was the prison-pen of the patriots as quickly as
possible.

The fact that he walked quite fast saved him from being
assaulted a much longer time than would otherwise have
elapsed. Moggsley was surprised at the speed at which the
youth was going.

"What in blazes is he up to?" he asked himself. "Why
is he walking so fast? I wonder if he has discovered that
he is followed?"

This thought gave the scoundrel some uneasiness.

He was a coward at heart, and the thrashing Dick
had given him the night before had inspired him with a
wholesome respect for the youth's prowess.

If the youth suspected that he was being followed, and
was on his guard, it would be a difficult and dangerous
undertaking to attack him.

Moggsley was desperate, however, and gritting his teeth,
he hastened after the youth, and gradually drew nearer to
his intended victim.

Dick really had no thought that he was followed, but
he had a splendid hearing, and as he was walking rapidly
along, he heard a noise behind him.

He whirled quickly.

He was only just in time.

As he whirled, he saw a dark form coming toward him.

The form was that of a man, and was only a few feet

distant.

Instinctively the youth knew someone had followed him from the camp, and he felt that it would be a fight to the death.

He had splendid eyes, and possessed the cat-like faculty of seeing after night—not to the degree possessed by the members of the feline tribe, of course, but to a degree more than the average human being—and he detected the flash of steel.

He reached up and grasped the wrist of the arm, in the hand of which was, he was confident, a knife, or weapon of some kind.

Having got hold of the wrist, the youth held on firmly, for he knew that his safety lay in doing so.

His assailant speedily proved himself to be no mean opponent, and the struggle which was waged there in the darkness was a terrible one.

Not a word was spoken.

Breath was too precious to be wasted in that manner.

Backward and forward, around and around the two moved, each striving to get the advantage of the other.

Dick was a skilled wrestler, and was as hard to get off his feet as a cat. Moreover, he was more powerful than most men, and his assailant had his work cut out for him.

Suddenly, in moving about, Dick's foot caught in a vine or something, and although he made an almost superhuman effort to keep from falling, he could not save himself.

Exercising his cat-like faculties, however, Dick, in

falling, managed to make a quick twist and reverse movement, at the same time turning his assailant's body half way around, and the result was that when they struck the ground Dick was on top.

A peculiar, gasping groan escaped the fellow, and Dick wondered at it.

"Is it a trick to get me to let go of him?" the youth asked himself.

He held onto the fellow's wrists with a grip of iron for a few moments, and then as the fellow made no movement, nor tried to wrench his wrists loose, Dick became convinced that his assailant had been badly hurt in the fall.

One of the fellow's arms—the one in the hand of which was the knife—was doubled under his body, and Dick, possessed of a strange suspicion, made an examination by feeling about.

Suddenly he made a discovery:

The knife which the fellow had in his hand had got turned with the point upward as they fell, and he had fallen on it, and had been killed by his own weapon almost instantly!

A feeling of horror came over Dick, but he dismissed it as quickly as it came, almost.

"It is war times, and he would have killed me," he said to himself. "Self-defense is the first law of nature, and I but defended myself—as I intend to do under any and all circumstances, if I have to kill redcoats by the score!

My services are needed by my country, and I am going to live to be of service to the great Cause of Freedom just as long as I can!"

Dick wondered who his assailant was, and taking out a flint and steel, and gathering some twigs and dried grass, he struck a light and as his eyes fell upon the face of the dead man, he exclaimed:

"Moggsley!"

CHAPTER IX.

DICK TO THE RESCUE!

YES, the dead man was Moggsley, the soldier who had picked the quarrel with Dick the night before, and whom Dick had given a thrashing.

The youth understood the situation perfectly.

Moggsley, burning with a desire for revenge, had followed him, with the intention of murdering him.

He had failed, and had accomplished his own destruction.

"Well, served him right!" thought Dick, and extinguishing the light, he went his way, having first taken the pistols and cartridges off the dead man.

"He won't need them any more," the youth said to himself; "and I will put them to better use. I will use them in the service of my country."

One thing Dick was glad of, and that was that he could now be reasonably sure that he was not suspected of being a spy, and had not been followed for that reason.

Moggsley's incentive was hatred and revenge.

He doubtless had had no thought that the youth was a patriot spy.

Dick hastened on his way.

Every few minutes he paused and listened intently.

He feared he might have been followed by others Moggsley.

Such was not the case, however, and of course he did not hear anything more of an alarming nature from the rear.

Dick reached the beach presently, and paused.

"Now, how am I to reach the prison ship?" he asked himself.

He pondered a few moments.

"I can and will swim, if I have to do so," he said to himself; "but," he added; "I should think there would be a boat near here somewhere."

This was reasonable to suppose.

The prisoners would have to have food every day.

The food would have to be taken to them from shore.

Therefore, it followed that there must be a boat not far away.

"I'll find it," the youth thought. "It is close by, and I would be willing to wager that such is the case."

Dick hunted around, and was fortunate enough to find a stick, with a crook at one end of it in the shape hook.

Holding to the straight end of the stick, Dick walked slowly along the shore of the cove, dragging the stick along in such a manner that the hook would catch the rope chain holding the boat.

He had not gone far before he was stopped by feeling the stick held back, it having caught something pretty solid.

"That's the rope, I'll bet!" the youth thought, and feeling, he found that this was the ease.

"Good!" he murmured; "now to get aboard the prison ship!"

The youth climbed into the boat, untied the rope, and taking the oars, rowed slowly and carefully out into the cove.

He was careful not to make any more noise than was possible.

There would be a guard on the prison ship, and if he was heard he might get shot.

"I will have to be careful," he thought. "I don't want to fail now that I have gone this far and met with success. I must free those prisoners!"

Ahead of him he saw a light flash up and then go out again, and the youth slowed up, and moved very cautiously.

"That was the guard lighting his pipe," he thought; "I am close to the prison ship now."

And such was the case, for presently one of the oars struck against the hull of the old hulk.

It made a rasping noise that was heard on deck, for Dick heard a stir, and a voice exclaimed:

"What was that!"

Footsteps approached the side at a point almost directly e where Dick sat in the boat, and a voice cried out:

"Who comes there?"

Of course, Dick made no answer.

He sat there as motionless as a statue.

He scarcely breathed.

It would not do to be discovered now.

It would spoil all his plans.

He was determined to free the prisoners.

So he sat there as silent as the Sphinx.

"Hello! hello! I say! Who comes there?"

The guard's voice had an impatient ring.

Of course, Dick did not respond, and presently, after a silence of half a minute, the guard gave utterance to an exclamation of vexation, and walked away from the rail, as Dick could tell by the sound of his footsteps.

"A narrow escape!" thought Dick. "Well, I must get aboard."

He tied the rope to the rail, so the boat would not drift away, and then he listened, so as to locate the guard.

"I must overcome him first of all," the youth said to himself.

Then he thought that perhaps there might be more than one.

It would be best to investigate before making an attack

on the guard.

It would never do to attack one guard, and have three or four more leap upon him and make him prisoner.

Dick was brave, but he was cautious.

So he stole along the deck of the prison ship, and paused every three or four steps to listen.

He became convinced at last that there was but one man on guard.

There might be three or four on board, but the rest, if this was the case, were probably asleep.

Only one man was on guard at a time.

Dick located the guard, and stole toward the fellow.

The youth was glad the guard had lighted his pipe.

The faint glow of the fire in the bowl could be seen, and served as an excellent guide for Dick.

He stole forward, and being enabled to determine in which direction the guard was facing, the youth slipped around so as to approach the fellow from behind.

Closer and closer crept Dick.

He was almost within reach of the fellow.

"Blame such business as this!" the guard suddenly exclaimed, pettishly; "this is the dullest business I ever got into! Here I have to sit, with nothing to amuse me, while the boys over at the camp are playing cards, and telling stories, and singing songs, and having a good time. I like it where things are lively."

"All right; I'll make it lively for you, then!" said Dick, aloud, and then he leaped upon the startled British soldier, and bore him to the deck.

The fellow struggled fiercely, but it was no use.

He was a strong man, but Dick was stronger.

Then, too, he had taken the guard by surprise, and had succeeded in getting him by the throat.

This was a big advantage, for Dick squeezed the fellow's windpipe so tight that his wind was entirely shut off, and struggle as he might, the fellow could do nothing.

He speedily collapsed, and became unconscious.

"I am glad I didn't have to kill the fellow," thought Dick. "Now to tie and gag him."

Dick soon found a piece of rope, and bound the man's hands together behind his back.

Then the youth gagged the Briton, and rose to his feet with a sigh of satisfaction.

"Good!" he thought; "so far I have done very well. Now to see if the prisoners are aboard—but I know they are."

Dick made his way down the companionway, and went down the short stairway.

At the bottom was a door which led into a cabin.

Dick tried the door.

The knob turned, and he was enabled to push the door open.

The youth entered softly, and pausing, listened.

The sound of snoring came to his ears.

"Another guard, likely," the youth thought. "He must be a musician—he plays a horn while asleep."

Dick stole across the floor in the direction of the

snoring.

Soon he came to a door, and he knew that the sleeper was in a room adjoining the one in which he stood.

"I must have a light," the youth thought.

He began feeling about and presently found a table.

On the table he found a candle and tinder, and flint and steel.

In a few moments he had a light.

He looked around the cabin.

It was a room perhaps twelve feet square, but contained nothing of interest.

Dick's attention was attracted toward the door opening into the room whence came the sound of snoring.

"There's another guard in there, and I must make him a prisoner" he thought, and he stole across the room and tried the door.

It opened to his touch.

In a bunk at the side of the little room revealed to view lay a British soldier.

Dick did not hesitate.

He had no time to waste.

He leaped forward and throttled the fellow, quickly choking him into insensibility, and then tied him up as he had the other guard.

"I wonder if there are any more?" Dick asked himself. "I'll see," and he quickly made search.

There were several staterooms, but none of them were occupied.

"I guess there are no more guards than two," the youth thought. "Now to find the prisoners."

The youth looked around him undecidedly.

"I wonder where they would be?" he asked himself; and then he gave a start.

"Of course!" he exclaimed; "the hold! That's where I will find them!"

He took up the candle and began searching for the entrance to the hold.

He soon found it, and making his way down the ladder leading to the dark depths of the hold of the old, water-logged hulk, he held the candle above his head and looked about him.

The candle was insufficient to dispel the darkness of the hold, and seeing nobody, the youth called out:

"Hello! Is anybody here?"

"Who are you?" came back in weak tones from toward the end of the hold, where the darkness was most dense.

Dick made no answer at once, but hastened forward.

He was soon among the prisoners, and found that there were twelve of them.

They lay on their backs on the damp, slimy bottom of the hold, and their hands were tied behind their backs. Their ankles were bound also.

"Who are you?" asked one of the men, a man of forty years.

"I am Dick Slater, a patriot spy," replied Dick quietly, "and I have come to set you free!"

"Thank God!" went up from the lips of the suffering men.

Dick drew a knife from his pocket, and quickly cut the ropes binding the men's arms and ankles, and they sat up.

They could not get up, however, as they had lain there so long trussed up that the blood had stopped circuiting in the arms and legs, and it was nearly half an hour before the blood could be gotten into circulation again.

At last they were enabled to stand up, however, an walk about, and during the time they were doing this, Dick explained the situation.

The men were the two spies—one was named Bird, the other Thomas Harper—and ten soldiers who been captured by the British.

They were surprised to think that a youth like Dick accomplished so much, and shown so much daring.

"You took your life in your hands when you ventured within the British lines, my boy!" said Bird.

"I suppose so," replied Dick, simply. "I am ready to risk my life at any time for the sake of accomplishing something toward bringing about the freedom of the colonies."

"That is the way to talk!" said Harper, approvingly.

"Had you learned much that will be of benefit to our commander-in-chief before you were captured?" Dick.

"Yes; we had come in possession of considerable information of importance," replied Bird.

"If we can only escape now, and get back to New York to General Washington, we will be all right," said Harper.

"Have you learned anything of importance?" asked Bird.

"Yes; an attack is to be made on Brooklyn Heights within four days."

"Phew! say you so?"

"Yes."

"Then we must hasten back to New York and inform the commander-in-chief of this fact."

"So we must. Well, let us be going at once."

"We are only too glad to get a chance to get out of horrible place!" said Harper, with a shudder.

They left the hold, and entered the cabin.

The guard whom Dick had surprised asleep still lay where he had left him.

He glared at the youth and his companions with a look of murder in his eyes, but could not say anything, the gag preventing utterance.

"Good-bye!" said Bird, with a triumphant look. "We will leave you here, in your present condition, all night, and see how you like it!"

Dick now extinguished the candle and placed it in his pocket, and then led the way up on deck.

All was quiet there.

His presence had not attracted the attention of anyone save the two guards, and they were prisoners.

"Come," said Dick, and he led the way to the boat.

"The boat is small; we will have to make two trips," he said.

This was done, and half an hour later the entire party of patriots stood on the shore of the little cove.

"Hark!" said Dick, suddenly, in a low, cautious tone; "do you hear that?"

"It is the tramp of a body of men!" said Bird.

"It is a company of British soldiers!" said Harper.

"We must get away from here in a hurry," said Dick, and he told them to follow him, which they did, and he led them away at right angles, and as they got out of the line of march of the company of men, they paused and listened.

It was a body of British soldiers.

And what was more, they were in search of Dick.

He had left the camp two hours before, and not having returned, Captain Parks had become suspicious, and had sent this body of men to look for him.

Parks had at last become suspicious that Dick was, after all, what Captain Frink had accused him of being—a patriot spy.

"The captain said that if the boy was a spy, he might set the prisoners free from the prison ship," Dick and his friends heard one of the British soldiers say; "so we better go aboard and see if everything is all right there."

Then the party of British passed on, and Dick said:

"They will go aboard the prison ship and learn all within twenty minutes! If we escape, we will have to hurry, for they will arouse the entire army, and men will swarm about us like hornets!"

CHAPTER X.

THE LIBERTY BOYS IN BATTLE.

"THAT is as true as anything you ever said," said Bird.

"We must hurry!" said Harper.

"What direction shall we take?" asked Dick. "Shall we go around to the eastward, or in the other direction?"

"It is not so far to Stirling's outpost as it is to Sullivan's," replied Bird, "so I am in favor of going around to the westward, and trying to reach Stirling's division."

"Very well; we will go that way, then," said Dick; "you lead the way, as you are more familiar with the lay of the land hereabouts than I am."

Bird took the lead, and they set out.

They had not been moving along more than twenty minutes when there was an outcry in the direction from which they had just come.

"They have discovered the escape of their prisoners!" said Harper, grimly.

"Yes; and we will have to look out now!" said Bird.

It was evident that a general alarm had been sounded, for the little party of patriots soon found themselves in the midst of the British, and it was only by the exercise of great caution that they kept from being captured.

Once they ran almost into the arms, figuratively speaking, of a company of British, but the ready wit of Dick saved them.

"Have they found the escaped prisoners yet?" he asked, in well-simulated eagerness.

It will be remembered that it was quite dark, and it so happened that they were so far from the nearest camp fire that it was impossible for the British to see that they were not what they pretended to be—British soldiers like themselves. It was possible, only, to see the outlines of each other, and know that they were men, and that was all.

Dick's question threw the British off their guard and disarmed suspicion.

"No; they haven't found them yet," was the reply to Dick's question; "but we'll get them very soon. They can't get away."

"Oh, no; they can't get away!" said Dick, and the British captain failed to distinguish the sarcasm of the tone.

"You go that way, and we will go this," said Dick, in an authoritative tone; "there is no use of our going in the same direction."

"True; all right," and the company of British went on its way in blissful unconsciousness of the fact that its captain had talked with the escaping prisoners.

"Well, you have nerve, young man!" said Bird, admiringly; "I take off my hat to you!"

"That was a bold stroke!" said Harper.

"And like most bold strokes, it won," said Bird.

The little party hastened onward, and on a dozen occasions they were on the verge of discovery by the British, but they managed to escape detection till they were within half a mile of the American outpost, when they were confronted by a company of British, the commander of which ordered them to halt.

"Fire a volley into their ranks, and then run!" said Dick, in a low tone, and at the word he fired, the others doing likewise—they had found and repossessed themselves of their pistols before leaving the prison ship—and as exclamations of amazement and consternation escaped the British, Dick and his companions darted away.

They were quick, but so were the British, and they fired a volley after the fleeing patriots.

One of the patriot soldiers was wounded, but only slightly, and he kept on running.

They got away out of range before the British could fire a second volley, and kept running at as rapid a pace as possible, as they would not have allowed themselves to be recaptured now, when so close to the outpost of the Continental Army, for the world.

They were soon within the lines of Stirling's division, and as he was up, having been aroused by an orderly as soon as the fact was ascertained that something unusual was transpiring over within the British lines, Dick and his companions were taken before him at once.

Stirling was delighted when he learned of the escape of this little party from the prison-pen of the British, and he complimented Dick highly on the wonderful work which he had performed.

"It was not much to do," said Dick, modestly.

"It was a great deal to do!" was the reply; "and you have gained some important information, which will be of great value to the commander-in-chief."

"Yes, indeed!" said Bird.

"We wish to go right on," said Dick. "We must be at the headquarters before morning."

"I will furnish you three horses," said Stirling. "Then it will take you but a short time to reach your destination. The other men can stay here."

"We are from Sullivan's division," one said; "why not let us go on up there and rejoin our company?"

"That will be all right," Stirling said; "only you must be careful, and not allow yourselves to be recaptured."

"Trust us for that!" with a grim laugh. "They won't catch us again! We will fight to the death first! We have had one taste of British prison-pen, and we don't want another!"

Dick, Bird and Harper, mounted on good horses, were soon riding northward, along the old Yarrows road, and two hours later—they had to ride slowly on account of the darkness—they arrived at Brooklyn Heights.

They paused there long enough to put General Putnam on his guard, as they feared the British, now that the spies had escaped, might move on the Continental forces at once, and attack the Heights before morning, if they were successful in driving back Sullivan's and Stirling's visions.

"Let them come, if they want to," said Putnam with flashing eyes; "we will make it so hot for them, they will wish to go up into the Arctic regions to cool off!"

The spies left the horses there, and crossed over to New York, reaching the headquarters at about three o'clock.

It was thought best to report to the commander-in-chief at once, as in case the British decided to move on the American lines immediately, General Washington would wish to have information regarding the matter.

The great general was very glad they did report, and he greeted the three with delight.

"So you are back again, Bird and Harper!" he exclaimed, "and you, Master Dick! I am glad to see you!"

"We are glad to get back, your excellency!" said Bird; "and Harper and I owe our presence here to this youth, who penetrated into the British lines, and finally found and rescued us."

"Indeed! Well, well! I thought that perhaps he might succeed where men had failed, and that was the reason I sent him; but I did not expect that he would do so well as he has done."

Dick blushed at this praise, and tried to make out he had not done much of anything, but the commander-in-chief hushed him up.

"That will do, my boy," he said, kindly; "you have done a wonderful thing, and your work in this matter has been greatly to your credit. I will say that no spy of the Continental Army has ever done better work than that you have performed."

"That is absolutely true," said Bird.

Then Dick and the other two spies quickly put the

commander-in-chief in possession of all the facts in the case, and he decided to send reinforcements to General Putnam at once.

"Please send my company of 'Liberty Boys' among the others, your excellency," said Dick, and the commander-in-chief smilingly said the company of "Liberty Boys" should go, if Dick desired it.

Soon all was hustle in and around headquarters, and in the encampment of the Continental Army.

Three thousand troops were quickly on the move, Dick's company among them, and they crossed the river and reached Brooklyn Heights before the sun had risen.

The British did not move on the Americans that night.

Only General Howe could have told why they had not done so.

Doubtless his experience at Bunker Hill had imbued him with such a wholesome respect for the prowess of the patriots that he wanted more time in which to make up his mind.

Nor did the British move to the attack within four days, as Dick had heard several say they intended doing, when he was in the lines, and their reason for this was obvious: the British Army knew the spies reached General Washington with the information, and it was decided to delay attacking.

Dick and Bob and the other members of the company fretted at the inactivity.

They had come over from New York to the Heights in

in expectation of becoming engaged in battle with the British within a few hours, and as day after day passed and still the British held off, the boys became very restless.

"I want to fight!" said Bob Estabrook. "I want to get a chance to show the British what the 'Liberty Boys of '76' can do!"

All were eager for the conflict, and in their eagerness they got Dick to ask that their company be transferred to Stirling's division, it being a self-evident fact that the outposts should be the first to be attacked when the attack was made.

Putnam, willing to please the youths, he having taken a great liking to Dick, the boy spy, gave orders to have the boys uniformed and equipped, and allowed them to go down and join Stirling's division, and the youths were better sated, as they knew that they would be in the fight among very first, when the battle should begin.

But the British delayed attacking for days and weeks, and it was not until the twenty-seventh day of August that they finally made the attack.

The British fleet, under Admiral Howe, advanced and made a feint upon New York, while General Howe's troops advanced on the American outposts on shore.

The main portion of the British Army, under Generals Howe, Clinton, Percy and Cornwallis, made a night march, away around to the right, until they struck the Jamaica road, and when the other portion of the army attacked Stirling's and Sullivan's divisions, this large force was moving to attack the rear of Sullivan's position.

The force that was advancing on Stirling's division, and which came in sight just as the sun came up, was made up of the highland regiments of Scotland, and Stirling himself was a Scotchman.

"We are going to have a hard fight, my boys!" he said; "we will hold out as long as possible, however. Stand ready, and fight as men fighting for liberty should fight!"

A ringing cheer greeted his words, and it was evident that the patriots would fight like demons, before falling back toward the main body of troops at Brooklyn Heights.

Soon the attack began, and the "Liberty Boys of '76" were getting their first taste of war—cruel war.

They went into the battle with the enthusiasm of youth, however, and loaded and fired as rapidly as possible, standing their ground like veterans.

Dick was at their front and stood there like a statue, excepting when he was firing, when he became all life and action.

He fired rapidly, and cheered the boys with lively words of encouragement. He seemed not to realize that he was in danger.

And this was characteristic of all the members of the company of Liberty Boys, and they fought with the coolness and precision of veterans.

Stirling was here, there and everywhere, encouraging his men, and he noted with wondering admiration the brave manner in which the boys were fighting.

He spoke to them in complimentary terms, and was answered with a cheer.

The fire of the British was galling, and as they outnumbered the American Army greatly, they kept on advancing, even in the face of the terrible hail of bullets, and it became evident that the Americans would have to fall back, and retreat to Brooklyn Heights.

Stirling had just given the order to retreat in good order, when the British Army, under Howe and the other three generals above named, attacked the patriot army from the rear. The British had surprised Sullivan's division from the rear in the same manner, and had then advanced and fallen upon the rear of Stirling's division.

It was evident, now, that it was going to be simply a question of reaching the Heights as quickly as possible, and Stirling told his men to fight their way through, if possible, and escape.

More desperate fighting between the Americans and the British never took place anywhere than now. The Americans fought like fiends, and in the front ranks of the fighters, doing the work of double their number, were the "Liberty Boys of '76."

They did wonderful service, and earned a reputation then and there for personal bravery, for intrepid daring in the face of superior numbers, that remained with them throughout the entire war.

The majority of the patriot soldiers succeeded in

reaching the Brooklyn Heights, among them the "Liberty Boys of '76," but the brave Stirling himself was captured, though Dick, at the head of his company, made desperate efforts to prevent the capture.

The division under Sullivan—those who had escaped being killed—had already reached the Heights, and that same afternoon General Washington brought over several thousand troops to reinforce the Heights.

"If they try to take the Heights by force, they will be repulsed with great slaughter," said the commander-in-chief; but the British general had not forgotten Bunker Hill, and he was afraid to try to storm the works.

He settled down, instead, to make a siege, and General Washington, seeing that it would be impossible to withstand a siege, and realizing, too, that if the British should come around to the rear and cut them off from retreat, they would eventually have to surrender, quietly made arrangements with the owners of all the river craft available, and that night, under cover of darkness, the entire patriot army was transferred across the river to New York.

Next day the British were thunderstruck to find that their prey had escaped them. This feat, in which ten thousand troops, with cannon, stores, etc., got away from a virtual death-trap in a night, and without the knowledge of the enemy, is considered as being one of the most wonderful and brilliant strokes of generalship the world has ever seen, and it placed Washington at once at the top, ranking with the great generals of the world.

The commander-in-chief learned of the gallant conduct of the "Liberty Boys of '76," and complimented them highly.

"Ah!" he said to Dick, "if I had ten thousand additional troops made up of 'Liberty Boys' such as are the members of your company, I would cross back over the East River and drive the British into the ocean!"

Dick repeated the commander-in-chief's words to Bob and the other members of the company, and they were as proud a lot of boys as ever the sun shone on.

The "Liberty Boys of '76" were destined to do wonderful work for the great Cause of Liberty during the remaining years of the war.

THE END.

LANDMARKS YOU CAN VISIT TODAY

1. Plaque at 161 Sixth Avenue
    George Washington's headquarters
2. Brookland Ferry Landing
    Where George Washington's army escaped to New York City under the cover of night
3. Fort Greene Park
    Prison Ship Martyrs Monument
4. Old Stone House of Brooklyn
    The heroic "Maryland 400" stopped the British advance overnight, fighting almost to the last man
5. Prospect Park
    Site of the most intense fighting of the battle
6. Battle Hill at Green-Wood Cemetery
    Site of fierce fighting commemorated by several monuments
7. John Paul Jones Park
    The opening shots of the Battle of Long Island took place here
8. Fort Wadsworth
    This is where the British forces prepared to cross the Narrows and invade Long Island
9. Rose And Crown Tavern Historical Marker, corner of Richmond Road and New Dorp Ln
    Used by the British as their headquarters

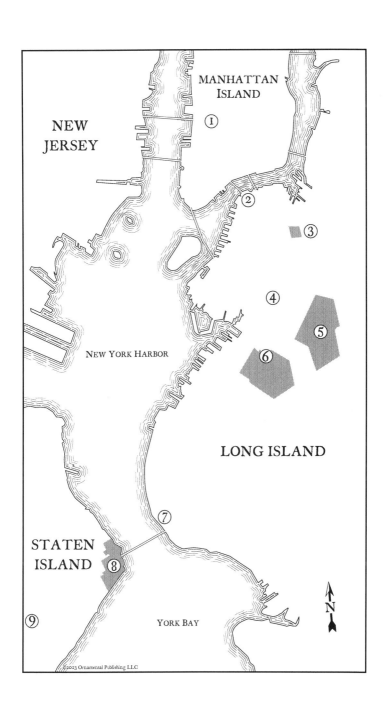

NEW JERSEY

MANHATTAN ISLAND

①

②

③

④

⑤

⑥

NEW YORK HARBOR

LONG ISLAND

⑦

STATEN ISLAND

⑧

⑨

YORK BAY

N

©2023 Ornamental Publishing LLC

THE LIBERTY BOYS OF '76.

Follow the adventures of Captain Dick Slater and his band of brave Liberty Boys as they battle the British Empire for American independence!

1. The Liberty Boys of '76;
   Or, Fighting for Freedom.
2. The Liberty Boys' Oath;
   Or, Settling With The British And Tories.
3. The Liberty Boys' Good Work
   Or, Helping General Washington.
4. The Liberty Boys On Hand;
   Or, Always In The Right Place.
5 The Liberty Boys' Nerve;
   Or, Not Afraid Of The King's Minions.
6. The Liberty Boys' Defiance;
   Or, "Catch And Hang Us If You Can."
7. The Liberty Boys In Demand;
   Or, The Champion Spies of the Revolution.
8. The Liberty Boys' Hard Fight;
   Or, Beset by British and Tories.
9. The Liberty Boys To The Rescue;
   Or, A Host Within Themselves.
10. The Liberty Boys' Narrow Escape;
    Or, A Neck-And-Neck Race With Death

WITH MORE TO COME!

Want more Liberty Boys?

www.thelibertyboysof76.com

Made in the USA
Middletown, DE
16 October 2023

40940929R00068